ABANDONED

GOVINDA SONTHALIA

Made with ♥ on the Notion Press Platform
www.notionpress.com

Contents

Contents

CHAPTER ONE

People began to pour themselves in the bazaar for evening snacks. Clad mostly in their best attire they greeted known faces, exchanged smiles or words, some genuine some pretentious. Few hugged out, few shook hands and few gave a nod. Those who conversed largely talked about work or politics or jewellery or attire. One thing that they all agreed upon was the heat.

The sun was almost done for the day, illuminating the sky with a shade of orange. It was hot and humid with no indication of any breeze. The cauldrons, large or small, in shops and stalls were put above fiery flames adding to the hotness of the surrounding. The whole area felt like being trapped inside a furnace.

Heat though criticized didn't stop the two or four legged stomachs with the aid of noses to push their masters in front of delicious food delicacies. Soon, all the shops and stalls had a large number of voices barking, either to hurry or demanding for more.

A large man emerged from the thick of the crowd, panting. "Auto," he said raising his right arm, signalling it to wait for him. He had hurried himself on a full fed belly to get there, not a wise decision. A series of burps came out of him and the heat wasn't helping. Drops of sweat trickled down from his hair, head and every inch of his visible brown skin. His peach coloured shirt had glued to his skin and his palms rested on his kneecaps, his face low and red and hot, still burping.

"Auto," he said once more after his body was calmer.

The auto stood still, like it had for a while. It had hung around its spot, saying no to any creature that made its way near it. Those that didn't like its response went blood red and gave it a mouthful of abusive words or an irritated expression. Two things were certain. First, the heat finally had taken its toll on all individuals, once their tummies grew a few inches, and second, the three-wheeler was on a world of its own.

Turning a blind eye towards the large man, the three-wheeler moved its black body a few paces where a skinny lad of eighteen had appeared. The boy smiled recognizing his ride. He threw open the curtains, tossed in his maroon schoolbag and hopped in. A brawl would have started if the large man had not turned his back.

The auto made its way up the bazaar until it greeted another lad of eighteen who seemed to have the weight of the world on his back. A girl of the same age was beside him, holding his hand. As soon as they got in, the auto picked up speed and honked its way out of the bazaar. On its way to Best Coaching Classes or as the villagers called BCC it picked up two more passengers, a boy and a girl. On reaching BCC the latter customers got off along with the skinny lad and the curtains of the auto was drawn tight. Then the black ride paced away under the dark sky for its second business.

To the right of the three-wheeler was the abandoned road, almost three miles from BCC. On either side there were large shaggy trees giving it a cave like appearance. Casually, the small circular wheels entered the route towards its second home. It went past by the cave followed by vast open areas that were mostly barren. A humungous banyan tree awaited the auto's arrival. The headlight went off and the tires stopped spinning as the auto took in to the shelter of the banyan tree.

"You have an hour to yourselves but first my money," Aavi said to the two passengers on the backseat of his auto-rickshaw or as he called it *Otto*. In the middle of nowhere Aavi's voice sounded thunderous and it struck the already scared teenagers like a lightning bolt. His muscular figure and messy hair formed a silhouette similar to that of a yeti.

Aavi drew away the curtains to let the natural light in and make him appear human. Once his pupils adjusted he saw the teenagers trembling in fear and excitement. They were still holding hands and their breathing was heavier, he could almost hear their heart beating in tandem. Aavi saw right through their shaky form. They couldn't wait for him to give them their privacy, a privacy that he and his *Otto* created. It was understandable and the feeling was mutual.

He didn't like being around people, it was a necessity. People who grew around him had the opinion that he was an introvert, they couldn't be more wrong. Acting like he belonged was not his style.

The sooner he got out from his *Otto* the better. Invading someone's privacy was the last thing on his mind or was any of his concern as to what anyone did. It all came down to the three hundred bucks he charged per ride and that was all that mattered. Payment always came first than anything else.

On second look, Aavi thought that these two were way out of their league to do anything. They looked like the kind who got picked on every day during an off period or recess. For them to carry on something like this must have taken whatsoever courage they had within them or that they couldn't keep it in their pants any longer. *Guess hormones does drive people crazy, even the little feeble ones.*

Small rectangular paper of three made up for his fee and went directly up into his shirt pocket.

"I will be back in an hour but if you need me early then call me. You have my number?"

Both the teenagers gave a quick nod of yes. Their eyes cried for his leave and their bodies couldn't wait to share their heat. *I'm going, I'm going.*

"One last thing, don't even dare to make a mess here or you will be sorry you ever trusted me." Aavi gave them a demonic look to let them know he meant it and then walked off.

The broken bridge was alone as always, waiting for him, calling for him and drawing him in. Aavi was the only one who visited or he liked to think so. The idea of anyone else coming here somewhat filled him with jealousy. It was his spot, away from the rest of the world. No people no judgement, only him and his thoughts.

Hatred and anger had driven him here so far off from his place and the village. This strange, broken and abandoned place slowly felt more like home than anywhere else. He usually came here after dusk and sometimes at dawn. Through, the last year or so, his visit was frequent since he started his second business. It was just a perfect idea. Although not a moral one but it paid handsomely.

Teenagers were always looking for a hiding place with their loved ones to express their love. In a place where love is considered a taboo and sex before marriage a sinister act there was too many watchful eyes to avoid. Many got caught to welcome their worst nightmare. Either a jealous ex or a so called concerned citizens or a neighbour reported their disgusting behaviour to the parents.

Unsurprisingly the girls had it rougher. Being blamed for provocation was the least of their suffering. The endless deplorable glare twined their hearts with guilt and shame. Confinement to one's house was always the first step and then, to be made invisible. Their existence was wiped out. Friends were no longer friends. They were either afraid of being associated to someone committing one of the greatest sin of all or simply were barred from keeping up that bond. In hindsight they were no more a living soul but an instrument to be used as befitted their parents who chiefly played their role upon the expectation of the society. Free will was a mere fantasy that enriched pseudo hope to their gloomy minds to pass the seconds, minutes, hours, days and years. What gave their existence value was their ability to turn their body into a vessel which ironically gave rise to the very society that condemned them.

Boys only had to face the red bubble of few expected faces and seldom got a few black spots.

Aavi, like all other souls, knew that a forbidden act was sure to get the most number of entrants. He had wrestled with himself over the idea of bringing the business here. One way or the other few or all of his customers could discover where they were and could just as well come here by themselves. The place itself was not a secret, everyone knew of its existence and location. It was left to isolation due to a stupid superstitious belief of the current older generation. Aavi was selfish of having to let go the desertion of this place which he thoroughly relished. On the other hand there was the temptation of earning easy money to which he finally caved in like a normal being. Luckily his risk bought him reward: money and no missing customers.

Like most of his evenings, Aavi laid on his back on the edge of the bridge staring at the sky. Right now it was a black blank sky, a total darkness. A darkness that had not only taken over the sky but spread out its wings all around Aavi. Trapped, blinded and all alone in this vast pitch black cage Aavi had felt like this for the most part of his life. No guidance, no relationships, no one to hang on to but himself. He didn't expect someone to spoon feed him but just a push every now and then to drive him out of his gloominess. For someone to even remotely achieve that would mean to understand him. Not that they wouldn't but the fact that he wouldn't let them. Therein was his dilemma. The way of the world wasn't unknown to him. He needed a brave soul to pull him out and fast.

Lately every day felt like a drag, seeing people together was not helping. Jealousy ignited in him on the sight of his evening customers. *Not so lucky after all.* His hands itched to squeeze or strangle them out of his *Otto*. Leaving them for the bridge only put him in a much worse condition, a state of sulkiness. A reason to live by was slipping; any purpose would do but what?

Wandering around this dark, dejected and rejected, a sudden light emerged in him. There were no chains here to bind him, he was somewhat free. It could be his world, a singular colour world and no variants. The very dark walls of this cage felt like a pillar now. He could do whatever he liked, be whatever he wanted, the possibility was limitless, an exciting prospect. How he would have loved if it were the same in the true world.

For a moment he was joyous, running around this dark like a spirited kid, buoyant. When his feet found the walls that protected him, fear crept in him. Beyond was the unknown and being discovered out there was scary. There were too many colours and even the shades of his were not his pals, all against one. Once they catch his scent even his muscular six foot figure trembled of the outcome.

The hour mark alarm clock Aavi had set on his watch set off. The colours of life were lurking around to pounce upon him.

CHAPTER TWO

Thud... thud.

Every single time! arghhhh... No matter how slow he drove or how cautiously, Misty had a knack for bumping his car along this rutted paved road. The ever so calm Misty grew red, clutched the steering wheel and shook it. He had had it today with everything going awry for him. From waking up late, missing breakfast, leaving his tie and papers at home, getting laughed at in his class, spilling his bottle of water and then tripping over it to know the woeful taste of mud. It was a day of these unintended events but one stuck out, striking his nerves and boiling his blood.

As expected, there was silence all around, no one ever drove up here and further. Woods he had left and woods formed his path. Miles before and miles further there was not a single town or village just trees and shrubs and open fields.

Regaining his calm Misty gave away a glimpse of disappointment, probably for losing his cool. The yellow light of the headlights followed up a curvy road and marked no intruders. It would have been the worst possible luck if there were to be any. Misty got out of his second handed Maruti Suzuki and stretched out his arms and legs. He had been driving for an hour and driving always gave him the cramps but driving was an absolute necessity. Though the sun had settled down hours ago the night didn't bring any relief. It was hot and the air stood still.

His past experience gave him the assurance to not check his prize though the prize today was nothing less than extraordinary. *A look wouldn't do any harm.* He unlocked the trunk of the car and stared at his win.

One of Misty's students, a boy of ten was curled up inside the trunk of his car. His hands and legs were tied up and a tape could be seen over his lips. The boy had given up the fight and strangely, was asleep.

Two hours of being in command with his evening pupils gave him the normality to his day. The fading sunlight then shined upon him. Mann the bold, the class prankster and joker stood at the back of the building of his tuition centre where Misty usually parked his car. When he met his eye the boy looked like how a ten year old should look, innocent.

"Why aren't you at home?"

Mann was busy fiddling a stone with his sandal. His teacher's question reached him but he chose not to answer. Grown-ups always needed to show their dominance, ordering or lecturing and beating when they needed to show who the boss was. He couldn't care less of what the teacher wanted. His back still ached from the slap his Dad gave him and though the red mark on his cheeks had faded a burning sensation still lingered. His throat felt heavy and he could burst out in tears at any given time. If he spoke, he was certain that he would blabber out all of his feelings so he chose to be a mute.

Misty repeated his question and got the same response.

Arrogant bastard...

He sat in his car and was ready to drive away when the day's itchiness caught up to him. The key dropped and he hit his head on the steering wheel in an attempt to pick it up. *To hell with everything, I need an act.*

It had been over a month since his last act. The acts took place on a random day but with months apart and never ever during festive seasons since the roads were busy and better patrolled. This dull period was a testament to his temperament and as always he was resolved to endure it. The hunger for the next act would build up the devil inside him, patiently flowing through him, filling him up with an enormous amount of pressure and dancing in his mind and heart to free it out. This beautiful game of being able to control it filled Misty with empowerment.

Rules are meant to be broken. Year after year of his monotonous method and routine it was time to break loose, to expand. Everything around him was almost perfect. Light had called upon its darker brother and the area was devoid of any artificial light. Trees formed the back of the building and to either side of the structure were small shops that closed early in this remote part of the village. To the front were large vacant areas that stretched far along either side. The only ones that could have seen Mann walking by were the shops to the left. Mann was still in his school attire so hours may or may not have passed since he came here. The shops to the left were the only ones that could have laid their eyes on Mann and they may or may not remember him. If, and it was a very gigantic 'if', that Mann's whereabouts questioning would come to him, Misty had the alibi of twenty students lecturing them.

In a matter of seconds Misty made his assumptions and came to a decision. Hurriedly, he threw the car gate wide open, got out and rushed towards Mann while calling him out. This time Mann gave a scornful look to his teacher which then turned to horror. Misty bashed his head to the brick wall while simultaneously cupping his mouth.

For a moment Mann's eyes widened with terror and he let out a muffled scream but the impact quickly rendered him unconscious.

When Misty was confident of the little brat being helpless, he released him. He ran his fingers through the boy's shaggy unwashed hair and felt a little bump on his head. No cut, no blood, no worries for him. The boy was unusually lightweight even for a ten year old. A body made up of feathers instead of bones. Misty carried him to the foot of the trunk of his car, dropped him, got the keys and shoved the tiny feathery fellow into the dark.

Later when his wife and daughter were fixated on the television he excused himself to the garage. This was an unplanned act so the ropes and duct tape were in the cabinets of his garage. Without further ado Misty wrapped up his present. The content wrapped up so tight that later when it came alive every movement inflicted a painful burning sensation as the rope grinded on the already deep red scars it had left.

After dinner he told his wife that a late night drive was long overdue and it would be wise if she didn't wait up. Before leaving he tucked his daughter to bed and kissed her a goodnight.

The Moon was shy to show itself, the stars weren't any better. Wind backed the clouds and trees to stay still. Birds weren't chirping, insects weren't buzzing and the engine wasn't running. Mann lay lifeless in the trunk. Misty's malice filled eyes were upon him with a wicked grin on his face. *You little brat, I am going to make you pay. Rest while you can you little rascal.*

The abandoned bridge, Misty's silent partner, stood firmly but half-broken. Over the past decade it had been what people might call his closest friend. All his fond memories traced back to the broken-bridge under its shelter. New happy memories awaited them both. He was the only friend of the bridge; he liked, wanted and prayed to think so. The silence that the bridge had to endure was all vanquished by his arrival. Before him all the bridge knew was betrayal, the warmth and the heat of the sun, the rain, the wind and the cold. Misty bestowed upon it the greatest gift of all, emotions of humans.

Misty stopped the car at the foot of the bridge. As he turned off the headlights darkness quilted everything. *Was ever a night as dark as this? Aha! This alone will scare the shit out of that brat.*

Misty turned on the torchlight on his phone and held it on his left hand, with his right he picked up the trunk. He was relieved to see Mann in a senseless state; it made the job easy not that it would cause any difficulty after all they were always kids. He had had his share of punches and kicks and they were nothing less than a mosquito bite. One wouldn't be hurt so much as annoyed.

Upon placing Mann on his left shoulder Misty flashed the torchlight from his mobile towards his lonely friend, signalling it of his arrival. There was a surge of energy all over Misty, an excitement lingered in the air around him. He marched on with this aura and approached the railing on the right side of the bridge. From there he took a sharp right, to the left were the steep slopes leading one down to the river. Misty ceased to walk when he reached a point where to his left the slopes fell less sharply, he took that route. The river that once boasted the prowess of its current to carry away any object now lay like a person in a sickbed. Years of minimal rainfall left this once soaring river with patches of sand, rocks and stones all over it. Misty took a left and strolled along the sand.

The base of Misty's operation was under the foot of the bridge. Against the slope rested a spade that Misty thought wise enough to be left here rather than carrying it around in the trunk of his car every time its need arose. Beside it was a small rock on which lay a set of ragged clothes. A smaller rock was placed on top of it lest the wind howled it over to an unknown area. He lay Mann there against the slope and took off to splash some water over his face.

It was time for him to draw all of his undivided attention to Mann.

A series of quick light slaps to Mann's right cheek awoke him from his slumber. It took a while for the ten year old to comprehend his situation. His head was spinning, his throat was dry and his stomach rumbled. When he realized his lips, hands and legs had lost its freedom, horror filled his face. The horror multiplied when he saw a figure in a squatting position facing him. The darkness withheld his kidnapper's identity.

Mann was not a little kid anymore. He knew what was to follow and what death meant. He decided that he was not scared of death. His mother was dead. She had died months after he was born, some kind of disease Mann couldn't remember. Maybe he would finally get to meet her in heaven, that's where everyone told him she was. Maybe she will shower him with love, Mothers are loving and kind or else all his friends wouldn't bring such delicious lunch every day to school. Finally, he will be able to call her Ma to her face and not to a passport size photograph that lay under the mattress of his bed.

Maybe dying was for good, no more of father's beating too.

Mann became terrified, his body shook in fear. To die he needed to be killed and to be killed he needed to be hurt.

He knew pain, he took a beating at home regularly and was regularly involved in a fight with someone. But this, right now it would be a pain of an altogether different kind.

A light flashed right through his face blinding him. Instinctively he shut his eyes but a curiosity erupted in him to have a look at the other person. When the light hit him no more he saw his Mathematics teacher. Hope ignited within him and all of a sudden he wanted to live and he didn't know why. He hated the subject and the teacher. Never would he have dreamt of seeing his Mathematics teacher and experience such tremendous joy. He thanked God and foolishly vowed to love the subject and study it with all his heart.

Misty removed the lips sealer and gave him the power of speech. Immediately Mann cried, "Sir, help me! Help me! Thank God you are here. Please Sir, help me!"

Misty was amused by this chain of reaction. For the first time ever he had a subject that he knew and it knew him. Past experiences had only been of conveying terror, fear and helplessness. This, right now, he had aroused hope, a new kind of rush entered his body. To his disappointment the night was no more a dark cover but Mann had not disappointed. When he gained his conscious the boy behaved like a mad fool looking everywhere and nowhere unable to figure out anything. He was sure that Mann even failed to notice him. It took all in him to control his laughter as he wanted the fun to continue. The way Mann's face went white all of a sudden he gained a moral victory. *Take that you brat! Enjoy life now!*

The victory was short lived. He anticipated Mann to cry, beg but Mann was like a statue holding his posture, lost somewhere else. His face was calm and he was clearly anywhere but here. Anger came over at once and he almost lifted his hand to thrash the boy back here. Misty then had a better idea.

"Sure I will help you my boy. Why do you think I removed the tape over your mouth?" *What a fool!*

"Thank you Sir, thank you Sir." Mann was overjoyed. He was going to be free.

"Are you okay? Are you hurt?" Misty said in a concerned voice and acted as if he really did care.

Mann deceived by his teacher opened up. "My hands and feet hurt, my head is spinning. I am so thirsty Sir, so thirsty."

"Ah! Don't worry. Wait here, I am going to fetch you some water."

Mann drank whatever Misty's hand held. In all his eagerness he even licked his teacher's hand. Misty didn't like that one bit but he put a big pitiful smile when Mann looked at him with doggy eyes. He rubbed off the saliva on the sand and said, "Come on let's get you out of here."

Mann followed like an obedient student. He clasped his teacher's arm and felt safe. Looking up to his teacher, his saviour, Mann found a hero in his life. All the disrespect he had shown to him in his class shamed him. "Sorry," he mumbled.

"Did you say something?" Misty questioned.

"Oh Sir, I was ... just .... I wanted to say I'm sorry for always misbehaving in your class." Mann's words almost got stuck in his throat. His throat was heavier and he hung his head down. He didn't have the courage to meet his teacher's eyes.

You had to say something. You had to make me remember, Idiot.

Misty was about to free his arm and smash the kid but the kid had loosened his grip. A gut feeling told him *he remembers.*

In a second Mann was off, running as fast as his little legs could. Thinking about his shameless behaviour towards his teacher brought back the day's earlier events when he was ignoring Sir Misty on the back of the building. His memory refreshed the scene when Sir Misty forcefully pushed his head back to a wall. Then he was here, alone and in front of Sir Misty. *Stupid! Stupid! Stupid!* Mann cursed himself. A familiar face had kindled false hope and covered the face of a perpetrator with the mask of a hero. Mann ran.

It was laughable for Misty for how easy it was to catch up with his student. The fact that they were in the open with no place for Mann to hide worked in his favour. The stars had aligned for him serving his prey to him on a silver platter. He was not ready to let all this fun go out. Whenever he came alongside Mann he took the time to fill his heart with Mann's petrified expressions and then hold himself back. It was all too easy.

Okay, playtime's over. Mann was crawling up the steep slope towards the forest. In a jiffy Misty grabbed and pulled Mann's ankles. Snap!

Mann lay on the sand crying out loud while holding his nose. Dark fluid oozed out from his nose, it had hit a stone and was now broken.

"Not so tough, are you?" Misty mocked him.

Five minutes it took Misty to drag back his subject under the roof of his friend. Mann all the while apologised, begged and pleaded. The kid's shrill voice was driving Misty crazy but he let him wail. The more he was annoyed the more joy it would be to let it all out.

Mann caught his teacher's legs in desperation asking for mercy. He knew his end was near and put on one last effort for his life. "Please Sir, please Sir let me go. I will never make fun of you in the class again. I will do as you say, I will keep quiet. I will not speak of this too." Mann screamed in pain as his teacher pulled his hair. "You are a MONSTER!!"

"I know." Finally Misty let out all the laughter that he had held back. This whole scenario was very amusing to him from the very beginning. Pretending to be the rescuer and for the victim to actually believe it was all very mischievous and wicked. *Why didn't I do this earlier?*

If there was a devil then it was here right now in front of Mann. When he saw the sudden burst of heinous laughter from Sir Misty no sight had ever frightened him so much. Devil, devil was all that came to his mind. No one was coming to help not even God. Mann accepted his faith. *Mother I'm coming to you.*

The adult hand was firmly around his neck squeezing the life out of him. He knew it was useless to fight but involuntarily his weak arms tried to free the tight grasp and his legs kicked the sand.

Blood rushed up Mann's face and he was all swollen. The Moon was back and shining. Misty could see clearly and it was a sight to behold. All the negativity of the past month and especially today's was flowing from all over his body through his hands. He was tightening his grip every few seconds and he could sense the end was near.

I HA...TE YOU were Mann's last words.

Little brat! The feeling is mutual. No more fart jokes.

"HEY!" A voice called out.

CHAPTER THREE

For the tenth time Aavi placed a call and for the tenth time the phone rang on the other end and for the tenth time the only answer he got was a disconnected beep sound. Aavi threw the phone on his bed in frustration and lay down. He closed his eyes, tried to get some sleep but it was of no use. His mind was preoccupied. Like a routine he picked up his phone and checked to see for any reply to the messages he had sent. No reply, no miss calls, nothing.

Aavi got to his feet and walked hastily from his room to the living room/kitchen to his Mothers back and forth, annoyed, wishing for her to appear out of thin air. He knew she was out and when she does come, it would be from the entrance door of the living room. He checked his cell phone again, nothing. It was almost midnight.

When he had come back home it was past eight. The windows were shut and no rays of light slipped through the bottom of the entrance. The door stood shut upon ringing the doorbell. He took out the spare keys from his pocket and let himself in. It was hot inside and smelled of sweat and cigarettes. He knew what the smell meant and it irked him. Quickly he opened up all the three windows to let the fresh air come in. After he freshened up and made himself dinner he glanced at his cell phone for any messages or call from his Mom that he may have missed. To his disappointment there weren't any. Patiently he waited for her till ten but she was of no show.

Aavi knew exactly what she was up to but they had a deal. She was to not go anywhere after dark. He trusted her but not men. What kind of weirdoes she might encounter at night, there was no telling. This though was not the sole reason or the important aspect of the deal and for that he was a bit ashamed. Safety was a priority but in her line of work, day or night didn't guarantee that. God forbid but if anyone wronged her it could be as easily at daylight as at night. Aavi couldn't get his Mom out of what she was doing. If he was making more money than her then she could have been persuaded. For her to continue and for it to be in his best interest, it would be better if it took place in his absence. She would still go on but there was a possibility of her sitting idly at home. If in his presence she was absent then it was absolute she was working and that would drive him from anger to madness. Hence, Aavi left early and came after sunset.

Somehow Aavi was not the least bit worried. Rather he was furious with her. Lying on the bed thinking about it grew his resentment towards her. Their relationship was all but over. Of course he cared for her but he couldn't stand the sight of her. Yet, now he couldn't wait to see her. They talked but it was all formal. *How's work going Aavi? Good. How's your health? Good. Did you eat? Yes. Do you need any money? No.* He started working because he didn't want anything to do with her money. All the questions were always from her side but tonight he sure was going to do all the questioning.

Right now, seeing that it was almost midnight Aavi was a bit bothered about his Mom's whereabouts. There were not that many people that had the courage to call her or be with her this late, this freaked him out. Either that person was someone powerful or a thug or crazy. Almost everyone in the village knew of her and her work. Daytime was easy for her to be called out or be visited. Men worked at daytime, wives knew it was work time and few prayed and kept faith that their husbands were at work. They didn't have it in them to call or check on their partners. But when dusk came men were to be at home. Anywhere else aroused suspicion for the flawed ones. If they were out, they were to be out with their wives.

A black SUV arrived outside Aavi's house. It woke him up. He had dozed off for a half-hour. The sleep was unexpected and that's how it usually happens when it evades one. He walked to his Mom's room and peeked through the open window. He wanted to take a glimpse of the person she was with. The person was not visible but he recognized the black SUV. There was no mistake and it was certainly bad news. *Of all people in this village she had to pick HIM!*

Aavi was getting impatient. He could hear his Mom fumbling with the keys. The black SUV was long gone. Finally his Mom entered and switched on the light.

"Oh! Dear God! You scared me. Umm... what are you doing up so late?" Reena asked.

"Are you drunk?" This wasn't the first thing he hoped to enquire but his Mom looked tipsy.

"NO."

"Ok, good. What are YOU doing out so late? Remember our deal!"

"Well were you worried about me?" Reena asked rather sarcastically.

"Yes." Aavi lifted his shoulder stating the obvious. *I AM your son. I will always be worried, no matter what!*

"So NOW you are worried about me. I thought you didn't want anything to do with me." Reena instantly regretted her words. She didn't know why she said that.

"You know what... do as you please. Go around and fuck the whole village." Aavi was fed up with his Mom.

Reena lost her temper and slapped Aavi right across his right cheek. "That's how you talk to your Mother?" Reena was all flared up. Her hair was all loose, her mascara was uneven and her cheeks were flushed.

Aavi was in tears, not from the slap but from how they had both reacted. He was out of line for a moment back there and that was not on his list of 'to say'. He looked at his Mom more in pity than hatred, she looked miserable.

"You have outdone yourself Ma. Enjoy the grave you have dug up." Aavi left right after. The door closed with a thunderous sound, not remotely what Aavi intended. *Otto* started and took off.

Reena was breathing hard. Her chest pumped up and down. She was still shocked with her sudden outburst. This had to be the first time she had ever hit her sweet Aavi. Her hands trembled. This had to be the first time she had ever hit anyone.

There was a mustard coloured couch in the middle of the room. Reena sat and lay back to take some respite. *How did it come to this?* She was definitely sorry for raising her hand but she lacked the courage to say it. One little word she had to say, it would not have made a hell lot of difference but could have meant at least something. She could have then calmed herself and talked to her son like an adult. Vow to not be out this late or promise to leave a message or something.

Reena's heart was still racing. She got up and drank a glass of water and returned back to the couch in her sorry state. The gold necklace felt like a boulder on her neck. It was a shiny and expensive piece of jewellery. A bit of a surprise took over her as Aavi hadn't taken a dig at it. She took it off, admired it and kept it beside her on the couch. She loved it and all the material value things she got from her clients but they were quite few. She mostly got clothes, shoes and cosmetics besides the money. Sometimes ornaments but jewellery was hard to come by. She had three sets of jewellery and they were all hidden in her closet. Neither those clients returned and luckily nor the jewellery with their angry wives. Those pieces though, were lighter and weren't that beautiful or expensive. Now she had a fourth set, sparkling like a king's crown and the giver was going nowhere.

This person was Shaanu, notorious for all illegal activities that were possible to be carried out in Uttampur village. Shaanu had an average height of five seven with a stocky figure. He had ebony skin and Reena's first impression of him was that he looked like a bull. Her contact name for him read as THE BULL. Shaanu's go to dress was a white *sando vest* with a *lungi*. His affection for gold was very visible with two thin and one thick gold chain around his neck. All his eight fingers had a ring on it, all gold with a coloured stone to display.

Two weeks earlier, around noon when Reena returned home after grocery shopping she had passed by a black SUV. At that time she didn't think it was waiting for her. Two men stood at her front gate that didn't look like potential customers but they had their eyes on her chest, *Rascals*.

"What can I help you with?" Reena asked with a customary smile.

The one with a childish moustache replied, "Are you Reena?"

"Yes."

The other fellow who appeared more grown up took out his cell phone and called someone. *She's here. Come around.* That's all he said on the phone.

Before Reena could question any further the childish one said, "Our boss wants you. You could go and change or something but don't take too much time. He has been waiting for an hour for you."

Reena was a bit confused but she shook it off and went in.

Ten minutes later her doorbell rang. From the peep hole she laid her eyes on a stocky ebony person covered in gold. *Money!*

"Myself, Shaanu," he said with a broad smile to display his white thirty two's.

"Reena..."

Shaanu dismissed his loyal dogs and led Reena to his SUV. After they were comfortably seated and the wheels took off he handed Reena four crisp paper valued at five hundred each. Reena had figured out that he was bad news but the money lit her eyes up. Shaanu in no time was all over her. The driver's presence was not welcomed by Reena but he had his eyes on the road. Looking was not prohibited as long as a certain amount was paid first.

They arrived to a place on the edge of the village obviously to keep away from prying eyes. His place was a single storey, cemented but not painted outside or inside. The place was equipped with things that could come in handy for them and nothing else. Reena was sure she wasn't the first one nor would she be the last.

Reena met him then each day at almost the same time. He would send a car to pick her up and drop her. As long as he was not abusive and violent she didn't mind. The money was pouring in and she somewhat had this notion that he would forbid her to see anyone else. It didn't happen which was a big surprise. The only thing he forbade her was to keep the sound of her phone on while his was more or less always buzzing. She didn't want to know or be involved in his business and she didn't let her curiosity get to her.

Today it was a bit different. She met him around the usual time and before they could get going he had to leave. Shaanu came back in the evening, rankled. He ignored her protests and took her to her room. Reena lacked the voice to say NO. They continued their fun back to Shaanu's den where he presented her a necklace that had Reena head over heels. Her eyes sparkled in gold and Shaanu told her she looked heavenly when she wore it. Reena was not a fool. The necklace wasn't new and probably belonged to his wife. She kept that to herself and didn't mind the gift.

Shaanu kept her late and ordered food. One of his workers brought it. After dinner he had another go and then they smoked for a while. For the first time he dropped her off and messed all her makeup in the car. It was past midnight; Reena figured her son was asleep and left her disarrayed appearance as it is.

Remorse was what Reena felt. She argued with herself of what was the use of it if she kept making mistakes. Moreover what was the use if she didn't learn from her wrong doings? It was a cycle that kept repeating, never deviating from its path. Anger, exchange words, guilt, quiet, less talk, mistake and repeat.

Change was what was needed, the positive kind.

For now Reena blamed the unexpected bombarding of her son's question and him looking at her in disgust and pity for her behaviour. A good outing turned sour.

When her nerves settled she went to bed, covered her face with a pillow and started crying.

CHAPTER FOUR

A furious Aavi sky rocketed *Otto* like a mad man to his secret place. The rash driving and the continuous honking didn't do a thing to let out the steam. If anything he wanted to slam something into pieces. It was déjà vu all over.

A decade ago, more or less, one fine morning Aavi as usual reached school on time. Aavi had grown to a muscular person the previous year. The daunting appearance kept the mischievous classmates away not that troubles came to his footstep before. When he entered the classroom two seniors were having a conversation with three of his classmates. They looked at him and enquired about something to one of the fellows from his class and the guy nodded.

"Hey," the senior said, "Your Mom's hot man. Does she...you know...in front of you..," then he made an obscene gesture, "She being a whore and all."

Aavi was fired up when the senior called his Mom hot and that gesture and the word 'whore' drove him beyond reason. First Aavi threw his backpack at that group and before they caught it he had lunged into the senior with the stupid big foul mouth.

They were both on the ground with Aavi on top. First thunderous blow from Aavi knocked few of the senior's teeth. One of his teeth pierced his lower lip and got stuck. Blood spilled from his mouth and he wailed like a baby.

Before the others could get to Aavi, he landed another monstrous blow tearing those thin boyish lips apart and now that tooth was stuck on his fist. Meanwhile the whole classroom went hysteric. Many were encouraging to strike and were starving to see more of those mighty blows and few sensible ones went out to bring in a teacher.

The group with the senior, all four of them, caught Aavi and tried to free their friend from his ravage. Aavi was strong but today he was unstoppable. His inner strength joined his outer and he carried on with his almighty blows. The senior was helpless like a slaughtered lamb. His body gave up after the very first hit it took and like an animal in a slaughter house waited for the butcher to finish the job.

The students realized that this had escalated way too far. The senior's friends were of no use. It was like a rat trying to throw out a gigantic rock out of its way. Others joined in and successfully separated Aavi from the almost lifeless body. Aavi was in a rage like none had ever witnessed and some of them had terrible drunken fathers who beat them or their moms. His eyes and face was blood red. Veins popped out from every part of his skin and his breathing was heavy. At that moment a fear of him was engraved inside every student in that classroom. It was very unlike Aavi, he was tall, broad and all but he stayed away from everyone. Quiet in or out of the classroom and helped anyone who asked and kept a decent grade. Didn't have any friends but was not unpleasant to anyone. Now nothing was the same anymore. The perception of Aavi to everyone had drastically taken a hit in those minutes. He was an ill-tempered and a violent individual. His quietness before all was an act to hide the evil behind his rough exterior. No one was ever coming near him again.

Three teachers rushed in followed by a few students. They took control of the situation. Immediately one of the teachers carried off the senior in his arms and rushed straight to the hospital. Another teacher drove the crowd away from the classroom and locked themselves out. The biggest of the three teachers handled Aavi. He placed his arm underneath Aavi's and brought it back of Aavi's neck and had him in lockdown. Aavi was being very aggressive, using his elbows and heels to fight back to his freedom. The teacher shouted on top of his voice near Aavi's right ear, "Stay STILL Aavi, stay STILL. You will only hurt yourself if you move, do you understand that? Now calm down. I SAID CALM DOWN AAVI!! CALM DOWN!! Take deep breaths. Yeah that's it, take deep breaths."

Aavi gave into his teacher words and the teacher released him. The blood rush to his head had him trolling around like a drunk, bumping a few benches with his hips and thighs till he sat down. When his senses returned Aavi was instantly disturbed by his actions. He was anxious to know what had become of that fellow so he asked to no one in particular," Excuse me Sir, any word on that senior?" He sounded regretful.

The teacher shook his head.

Aavi had no sense of how much time had elapsed since his unspeakable actions. Karma had wasted no time in bestowing its gift to Aavi. On a loop his mind replayed how he drew out blood like squeezing out ketchup. Things he hadn't noticed his subconscious had carefully wrapped it up and now displayed them in high resolution.

Even before he had punched, those sorry eyes pleaded forgiveness. They didn't shut themselves from the imminent danger but faced it regretfully. Second time the curtains were drawn. He could have ceased himself, the punishment was done and dusted but the crowds wild encouraging voices flared him up. A flame that was in ignition now raved and this time around it tore that paper thin lips. Aavi recalled a tooth being stuck on his fist. He looked, and sure enough, there was the senior's yellowish tooth dangling. If he hadn't comprehended the damage he had done the tooth was a harsh reminder.

The way Aavi had gone about this whole thing had left a big scar of hate in him for himself. Words, that's all what it was, a few words. True or false was insignificant. There was a variety of choices: could have ignored it or come up with a witty reply (Nope, there could be none here) or could have walked out. Deep down Aavi knew the truth of those letters. As far as back in time he could go either to the market to buy clothes or to the movies or simply for grocery shopping along with his Mom she was not spared from those lecherous gazes. Something in him refused to accept the reality. Hiding places were now but over.

A teacher called him out. Slumbered in his guilt Aavi didn't hear it the first time.

"AAVI," One of the teachers cried aloud.

"Ye...yes Sir."

"Let's go. Your Mom has arrived."

Aavi was in the headlines of everyone's lips. A juvenile walking around with a grotesque mouth did raise curiosity of onlookers. The village talk was largely the aftermath of the visit the victim's parents made to his home. He not only let himself down but gave a silver spoon to the people to harass his Mom. He had grievously punished her unknowingly.

The month of suspension followed up by a month of summer holidays could not have come at a better time. He shunned himself from the outside world. On the seventeenth day his legs dragged him for a walk. The fresh air nullified the negative looks and after a few more outings Aavi was back to himself.

On one such outing he decided to leave school at the year end and drive an auto-rickshaw. He was not going places with his studies and it was difficult to concentrate in a classroom that reminded him of his savage actions. Moreover he didn't want to live off his Mom's money after it was certified how the money came.

Surprisingly that night yielded no arguments. His Mom raised no brows or questions, her face showed no indifference upon encountering Aavi's words of leaving school and being an auto driver. She gave him the funds he required. Money that he didn't want but still needed one last time.

Last day of his academic life was a harsh cold day. The wind howled all around freezing up any exposed skin. It was an uphill task to put pen to paper. Leaving an empty sheet for the teacher would not bring any reaction or consequences but Aavi was a diligent person. Finally when there was no use of ink, his feet acted on its own.

The bench that was warmed wasn't missed. Aavi was happy, happy in his *Otto's* cold seat and happy to inscribe a whole new storyline to his coming days.

Nothing lasts.

Driving and honking around Uttampur, *Otto* took him where his ignorant mind was to be enlightened. The clock turned backwards to the time when he was adjudged dangerous.

"GET IN," Aavi shouted on the top of his voice while pointing towards his vehicle. "I SAID GET IN."

Reena was dumbfounded. One moment she was going about her business and next a slight tweak in the day tweaked her fate to an uncertain corridor. Caught with her son's school principal added the right spice to inflame the tongue. Worse he had his hand at an inappropriate place in public. Aavi had taken up a fiend form that sent ripples throughout her body. His heavy irate voice crushed her eardrums and her own form trembled. She somewhat imagined the hellish circumstances it had been for that toothless senior student.

"GET IN NOW!" Aavi's voice thundered.

Reena's body stopped functioning. She desperately wanted to move, change her position from those big angry bulging eyes and flared nostrils. Her system refused to obey her mind since that piercing voice froze her all up.

Aavi's patience had run its course. Swiftly he strode up to his Mom and held her hand firmly. He dragged her up to his auto and pushed her to the back seat not before giving a fierce glare to his principal who being panic stricken lost his static balance and felt a faintness coming over.

Otto bore the wrath of its master. Pits or solid objects weren't given any consideration and instead of being avoided, they were run over. The dense white fog blurring the way made no reasonable protest to limit the speed as *Otto* was whizzed up the road.

The strong cold wind that slashed skin to skin all around failed to impose its sharpness on this driver and its passenger. Each more disturbed than the other for different reasons. Aavi was in disbelief of his stupidity. How could he possibly be so naive about the leniency of his one month school suspension over such a grave crime? How could he have not contemplated the reason for it? He may have grown physically, mentally poooff!!

Days that followed the suspension he had his head down in regret filled with remorse, expecting a soul to confront his pity state. What a fool was he? All cause of his Mom! In his mind he cussed her over and over again. His thumb giving away his temper as it constantly pressed the honk button.

Reena knew not how she could possibly confront her son and ease up the matter. What could she possibly say? There was no excuse. If anything Aavi should have put two and two together long before. Obviously he didn't, evidently for not having to face this scenario. He was at an arm's length with his back to her yet she didn't have it in her to call or put a hand on his shoulder and apologise. All she pictured was his hurt countenance reminding her of how she embarrassed him.

Otto made all the noise as the living sat dead.

After dropping of his Mom to their home Aavi sped off without any destination. They were yet to exchange any words or face each other.

This time *Otto* was being driven up more wildly and harshly. It was more like *Otto* was a layman riding an uncontrollable feral stallion.

A shaky and shivery Aavi turned off the engine and stepped out to a lonely road. It was dead quiet and as far as his vision could go not a light twinkled or approached. To either side of the road all there was, was, timber and supposedly greenery. The only sound that came was from the rustling of leaves.

Aavi put his arms across his chest and walked away to wherever the road headed.

The water ran downstream steadily. Standing on the edge of the bridge with his arms wide spread Aavi took deep breaths. He was soaked up from the humid climate even though it was past midnight. He wanted to forget everything mainly his Mom and her latest admirer Shaanu. Aavi had half of his foot in the air and toyed with luck by leaning forward. Surprisingly neither his heart raced nor his eyes flinched. The broken bridge had this soothing effect on him from the onset of its discovery.

Aavi stood there for a while before he noticed something unusual. On the far opposite end under the other part of the broken bridge there was a silhouette in a squatting position. First he mistook it for a vagrant going on about his business then he heard a cry; sharp, shrill and loud. His body lost grip and he almost fell. Someone was in trouble and pain. He had to help.

Aavi rushed back to find a way down. The slopes were all but vertical. He searched for something less vertiginous when another painful cry made him throw his body down. Rattling he went knocking up his palms. Soon, he was up and running towards the silhouette until the diminished water body got in between.

A man had his hands around a child's neck that gasped for breath. Aavi neither spoke nor protested till he heard the child stutter, ' I hate you.'

Mann's fate could have been different if Misty and Aavi hadn't been so preoccupied with themselves.

CHAPTER FIVE

"HEY!" A voice called out.

Misty got goose-bumps. *Shit!* He was in a fix and couldn't decide whether to make a run up the slope to his car or face the eminent threat. Of all the effing places to be caught this had to be the most unpredictable one. He scowled at Mann's faded face. *You degenerate wake up! I want to do it all over again. I want to tear you apart limb by limb. Couldn't let me have some peace and enjoy my victory could you?*

That deep and manly voice still rang in his ear. Misty was petrified. He so wished his method was crueller. A blade would have given him an upper hand. Then he heard a splash and turned impulsively.

An enormous broad bloke faced him and sent chills up his veins. *Oh dear! I'm screwed. How am I supposed to put up a fight to that!* That imaginary razor really would have come in handy.

Misty was a child murderer, the worst of the killing kind. Generally the magnitude of hatred for the other kind of killer was lesser in comparison. This was his end.

No! This is not how I die. Running away had slimmer chances than picking up a stone and smashing the big footed. *I could dash with full force of my bodyweight and strike his head on a rock or something.*

Meanwhile Aavi tried to make out the killer's face. The moon was up and above and ahead of him making it difficult. A child lay dead and there was no sign of any liquid gushing out from the still body. *Strangled to death? What kind of a person goes about killing someone so innocent? What could that child ever have done to drive him to this?*

Aavi had never seen a dead person before. Here he was now, a witness. The scenario was confusing. It was his moral duty to apprehend the killer and hand him over to the police. Then there was the possibility that in the process he could easily hurt the guy which the society would rather applaud. What troubled him was that at the end of this capture he could very well turn a killer which again the society would cheer, not him.

The short lean murderer was not a challenge given he had no weapon. Aavi proceeded forward.

"WAIT." Misty shouted. "You don't need to do this. Turn around and walk back. You never saw me and I you." Misty tried to keep the alarm out of his voice.

"I did and I can't."

"No, you can and you will. I don't want another life on my hands." Misty put on a brave bluff.

"You are tiny and short. I will take my chances." Aavi was rather cocky.

"You will regret it." Another poor bluff.

"I can hear the fear in your voice." Aavi had him.

Shit!

"Wait... wait... wait... wait... wait... wa... I know you!"

"No you don't."

"Yes I do...umm... Rohan, no, no, umm wait Mohan."

"The light is not bright enough for you to know. Don't delay the inevitable."

Misty needed to guess a right name. What he was hoping to accomplish he had no clue. He went along with whatever came to him.

"I will give you an option. Give up and come to me with no harmful intention and I promise I won't lay a finger on you. Else, I will hurt you and I mean it." Aavi stated.

Come on, come on, come on; think of something or this is it.

Misty then got a clear view of the hunters face. *AHA!*

"Your name is Aavi. I got you." Misty was overjoyed.

How does he know my name? "I'm not the only being with that name."

"You went to Uttampur high school." Misty shared his knowledge.

My school too! "Almost everyone attends that school."

"Remember that senior whom you knocked toothless and senseless?"

He definitely knows me. "So you know what I'm capable of. Just hand yourself over." Aavi was annoyed. This was not a quiz contest with a rapid Q&A round. It was an arrest.

"See Aavi my friend I am at an advantage you cannot even begin to fathom. THIS... HERE... is now in my favour. I guarantee I am walking past all this without a scratch," Misty said confidently.

"No you are not." *He does sound optimistic.*

A very broad grin lit up Misty's face. He was self-assured. *Huh! What a turn around. He has no idea how wrong he is.* Misty crossed the significantly diminished water body up to Aavi and whispered something.

HOW? Aavi turned yellow and pale. He had him for sure. *How was this possible? How could he have known? Lucky break or not I'm at his service.*

"I told you. Take your time, we aren't going anywhere." Misty retracted his steps and started humming some of his favourite lines.

Aavi sat on sand and stone in disbelief. His heart was pounding in fright and his body lost its stability. He felt awful and his body temperature rose up. His stomach wrenched and he spewed. A dead body hadn't taken that much of a toll on him. It was startling and bewildering.

Minutes later Aavi took a glance at Misty. He was having the time of his life, kicking and cussing the dead body and laughing in a deranged manner. Then he glanced at him.

"Come on, get up. Trust me I am not a tattletale. I have known you since school. Have I publicized you? No I haven't and will not. Don't sit there all gloomy and defeated, rejoice with me on my victory and I promise to wipe off that sadness. Now get up and join me." Misty pleaded with his hands.

Aavi sat dejected.

"Oh how rude of me to not even introduce myself. I am Misty, your pal, schoolmate and keeper."

Misty on noticing that Aavi wasn't paying attention and was rather lost in his misery like a sick fellow, came up to him and said, "Maybe this will ease things up." He whispered something more to Aavi.

That's how he knows my colour. He is the same not a variant. I'm safe.

"Christmas has come early for you. We have nothing more to hide from each other. You KNOW me and I know you. Now rub off that depressing show and enjoy this night." Misty was dancing up and down like a nincompoop.

That foolish dance made Aavi smile, he immediately withdrew it. Misty didn't miss it.

"Here take my hands, take it." Aavi took it and Misty pulled him up on his feet. "That wasn't tough was it?"

Aavi shook his head. He was suddenly Misty's follower.

"Now flail your hands and legs like a madman and let everything out."

Aavi joined Misty in his savage routine. They gave up control of their body and emptied their mind, both swinging and flinging themselves wildly till they were completely worn out. They shared a laugh once they rested flat on their back.

There was total silence for some time before Misty said, "We got to bury Mann."

"Who...?" Aavi questioned while gazing at the stars.

"The boy I killed." Misty was happy that he had to remind Aavi of it.

"Oh that." Aavi didn't know what to make of this. Guilt eluded him. Here he had run off to escaping the morality of his Mother's judgement while presently his own was put to test.

"Don't think too much." Misty broke Aavi's pensiveness. "Aavi you don't even know the kid and no one's gonna miss him. His Dad's a drunk, most likely an abuser and his Mom's passed too. I have done a favour to that kid."

"That's no reason to kill and there are plenty of kids facing that every day."

"Guess I have to find them all and free them from their despair. Would that do the trick?" They burst into laughter.

"It's going to get blue soon let's hurry up. I have to rush back to my wife and kid."

On hearing that Aavi's eyes popped out and he exclaimed, "YOU have a wife and kid!"

"Oh Yeah, been happily married for seven years. Isn't that genius of me or what?"

"How can you face them after what you just did?"

"This isn't my first rodeo pal. Also leave that to me."

"What about your wife? Has she not suspected you?"

"Not in any case."

"How do you explain your late night out?"

"She knows."

"What does she know?"

"That I sometimes go out late at night."

"She permits you."

"I'm not a child. I can do what I want."

"Do you give her a reason?"

"She thinks I am off to enjoying a long night drive."

"And she believes you?"

"Obviously or I wouldn't be here would I?"

"Hmmm..."

"Enough with the questions, we can discuss our lives later. Let's bury that little rascal."

"You hate that kid?"

"With all my heart..."

"One last question..?"

"Hit me."

"How do you know the ... O ... sorry ...knew the kid?"

"He's my student."

"I regularly visit Uttampur High School and have never seen you around."

"I don't teach there, I teach at Chaanpur High School."

"O. You live on the other side?"

"Ya..."

"How far is it from here to your place?"

"An hour and a half from here, the road's an accumulation of pits else it would take an hour only."

"Aren't there any villages in between?"

"No."

A flock of birds flew across the sky warning Misty to finish up the job. Misty stripped and took out the worn out clothes beneath the little rock.

"Why change?"

"Don't want to get these dirty?" Misty pointed at his stripped ones.

"You brought extra attire with you?"

"Long time back and these are dirty as hell." Misty grabbed the spade resting against the slope and said," Don't just stand there like you are in an assembly, grab the kid and follow me."

Misty took off to find a spot with Aavi behind him carrying Mann on his right shoulder.

"How long have you been doing this?"

"About a decade or so, It..."

"How many more have you killed?" Aavi interrupted.

"Twenty, thirty...uhhh... I don't know. I don't keep a track or record."

"All kids?"

"Uh-huh"

"And you have got away with every one of it?" Aavi's curiosity arose.

"Yes."

"Wow!" Misty's straightforward answer was making Aavi bold.

"Tell you my secret?"

"If you want to..."

Aavi dearly wanted the answer. The non-hesitant honest replies intrigued Aavi.

"Not today."

Misty stopped and threw the shovel up above the slope on solid ground and said, "Climb up, we will bury him there." They quickly climbed up on the gentle slope. "Drop the bastard here and take a rest. I am going yonder."

Aavi put Mann down and looked at the tiny, young and cold dead body. *I am sorry I wasn't and cannot further be of any help. Please forgive me.*

"Aavi, Aavi..." Misty called.

"Ya..."

"Help me out here." Misty saw Aavi's head tilt to the body and wasn't letting him develop a conscience.

Aavi and Misty took turn in digging up a grave.

"What were you doing up here in this abandoned place?" Misty asked.

"Nothing; happened to be here by chance."

"Don't lie."

"I'm not."

"Past midnight you woke up hot, cussed the weather and took off to cool off. On this expedition you wandered off miles to a forbidden place just to experience a cooler atmosphere. Mmmm that's some serious reason, I believe you."

"Sorry."

"Now reply honestly."

"I had a fight with Mom."

"Why?"

"A difference in opinion..."

"Elaborate."

"I don't want to. I don't think I can. I am in a better place right now."

"Need I remind you what you are doing right now?"

A collective HAHAHAHAHA echoed.

"That was rude of me, wasn't it?"

"Nah don't beat yourself up for this rascal."

"You have turned me into an accomplice." Aavi blamed Misty.

"What choice did I have? It was either that or be arrested or killed."

"I shouldn't have driven up here."

"You shouldn't have but I am glad."

"Are you?"

"Hell yeah... You know how difficult it's been for me all these years? To not share my most prized experience with anyone. It's not like I can go parading on the street with a banner detailing my kills or braying it to my wife. What's the point of being perfect at something without a soul to see it? A little appreciation is always a boost and welcomed."

"You are insane."

"Ahh..." Misty chuckled. "Then I have the workload, it's tiresome and woooo the loneliness it gets to you. With you as my partner things will get considerably better, easy and fun." Misty shared the truth but not all of it.

"I'm not your partner, this is a one-time thing," Aavi said in a dismissive tone.

"Are you sure? You seem to have forgotten who here has the upper hand."

"You will use that just to turn me into a killer?"

"I won't."

"Then what's your grand plan?"

"I will do nothing and yet you will show up."

"What do you reckon I am, an idiot?"

"No but I know you more than you can fathom. I haven't thought of you these past years until today after recognizing you. I have recollected some wonderful memories and they my friend has let me devise something wonderful."

Aavi felt scared. *What could he possibly know now than what was so deeply hidden? What more is there to me that*

I too can't figure out? These killers have always been able to outsmart people. There is a reason why they aren't easily caught. And why can't I recall him even a bit? Misty... the name too doesn't ring a bell and here he's talking about me like we were childhood buddies.

"All done, drag that brat for his decomposition." Misty said. The grave was ready to take in the dead.

Aavi buried Mann while Misty rested against the trunk of a nearby tree.

"What a day this has been wooooooooo," Misty said exhilaratingly, "It all seemed to fall apart, annoying me beyond words. If not for the kid I think I would have laid it all out on Drishti, my wife. God! He saved me from a volcanic disaster. I ought to thank the kiddo. How ironic? Deaths supposed to bring grief. Here it has relieved me from my stress and aligned my stars with yours. Damn the kid's on a streak here." Misty burst into laughter.

"Are you sure this won't come back to haunt me?" Aavi wasn't paying attention.

"Only thinking of yourself, Aavi? Spare some thought for your new pal."

"I'm serious. Won't his friends notice his absence?"

"O! I'm sure the ten year olds will bang every neighbourhood door demanding the immediate release of Mann. When results will fail a massive uproar of protests will be led out on the Chaanpur streets. This mob will break into the police station demonstrating their anger on the neglected and failed duty of the officers. All along media personnel following them, interviewing their classmates and providing regular updates to the adults watching their daily news. Then..."

"Okay STOP, I get it." Aavi was aggravated.

"Good. Now finish up."

Misty changed back while Aavi waited. After he placed the rock on top of the dirt worn out clothes he said, "Give me your phone."

"Why?" Aavi was still upset for being treated harshly.

"To exchange numbers."

"I don't want to."

"Are you ever gonna say yes to something. All I here is NO NO NO NO and then some more NO NO's."

"Don't talk to me like that."

"Ok there's no need for hostility." Misty recalled the hospitalized senior. He had not one chance of survival if he were to irate Aavi. "I'm sorry ok. It's been a stressful day. If it was anyone and I mean it anyone but YOU I probably would have drawn my last breath. Thank YOU Aavi for being here and I'm really sorry. Will you accept my humble apology?"

"I can do that."

"Yes you do that and let's start afresh. Phone please....pretty please."

Aavi couldn't help but smile on seeing Misty all goofy. "Here." Aavi gave Misty his cell phone.

Misty rang himself and wondered from where the ringing tuned out. "OH! It's on my car. Nearly felt sick." A sense of paranoia had caught up to Misty but he relaxed once the harmless danger was avoided. It had to be his most cowardly display in these few hours.

"It's amazing you haven't been caught."

"I KNOW!!"

"It's extraordinarily astonishing that a ... someone like you has the valour to go through picking up and killing little kids."

"Now you are just getting back at me." Misty was thankful to Aavi for not using the word coward. The word when directed at him, irrelevant of the circumstances, sparked a hatred for any vocal that spoke it. Regardless of how truly it characterised him that verity was a bitter pill to swallow.

"I think I have earned that right."

"I did overreact then. After my first act... you know the first time I throttled I perspired like a fatso and that too on a chilly night. I wasn't married then so at least I didn't have to face a known face. I was worried like a disease had clung to me and refused to leave. A week passed and the absence of any reports or rumour of a killer in the midst composed me down. It's only natural that you would enquire for your safety."

"Hmmm"

"Let bygone's be bygone."

"Ok."

"I will text you and expect you for our next meet."

"Please don't involve me anymore. We can talk but I have had my share of sinful activities. You are free to continue to do what you do and I won't interfere or rat you out. I'm sincerely done."

One moment he is authoritative and the next he's pleading. What a fickle minded person you are Aavi. Good. You continue to shower the chips on my table. Thank you God!

Misty didn't respond and Aavi stayed silent.

"I better be going, bye," Aavi said.

"Wait one last thing."

Misty went up to Aavi and their colours fused.

CHAPTER SIX

"Hello daddy."

"Hey!" Misty exclaimed on being greeted by his kid Tia. "What are you doing up so early?"

"I... woke up....daddy. Your car came... ghrrr ghrrrrr and I woke."

"Oh Daddy is sorry for waking his little angel up." Misty closed the door behind and locked it.

"Where you Daddy..?"

"Daddy was out."

"Why?"

"Cause Daddy can."

Tia stared with her big black googly eyes. Her dark hair a batch of loosely jumbled up springs. Unable to process up a response she pattered with her tiny feet towards her Dad. The silver anklet jingled. She had her arms wide open inviting her Dad to pick her up.

Misty lifted his five year old with ease. She was royally held around his left arm. A series of tickles to her belly struck a chord of laughter.

"Shhhhhhhhhh... Mommy is asleep." Misty gestured a sleep sign and his daughter imitated and giggled.

"Daddy smells..."

Uhh I stink. Misty put Tia down and ordered, "Go back to bed and sleep."

Tia marched back obeying her Dad instantly.

Chapattis, fried potatoes and tea were placed on the table for breakfast.

"What time did you get in?" Shreya, Misty's wife, asked as she took a seat. Drishti was fictional.

"I don't know two, three. I was too tired and went straight to sleep."

"And you are up early."

"I'm up early."

"You didn't hold me last night."

"Like I said I was tired." Misty usually held her to let her know he was home.

"I don't know why you torture yourself with these late night drives."

"When I know the answer to that I will tell you myself."

Apart from Tia striking her Dad with potatoes and Shreya gently breaking away Tia's play they ate in silence.

Chaanpur High School was located at the heart of Chaanpur village. It was twice the size of Uttampur High School and so was Chaanpur compared to Uttampur though they both attracted crowds and students from their surrounding neighbours. Misty parked his car at his usual spot and got out with Tia.

They made their way through a trickle of young boys and girls who all wished Sir Misty a 'Good Morning.' In response he nodded a few times. After dropping Tia to her classroom Misty took to his class. He had to teach the first, second, fourth and seventh period today.

Another 'Good Morning Sir' but in chorus welcomed him. Misty placed his bag on the teacher's desk and took out the attendance register. It was customary for the first period teacher to take the attendance of their class.

Misty called out the names of the fifth standard students. Ticking the present and crossing out the absentees.

"Mann."

No response.

"Mann."

No response.

Misty eyed the fifty odd boys and girls searching for the one called out. Absent. Mann was crossed out.

"Take out your books and turn to page 28. Today we will learn factors."

At the end he asked the class for the whereabouts of the five absentees and none knew about Mann. *That pig. No one even cares. Good riddance. Perfect.*

Aavi's neck and back ached. Pondering about last night's events and decision-making his exhausted body and mind propelled him to sleep at the back seat of his *Otto.* It was around noon before Aavi rose. It was sultry as the day before and beads of sweat poured out from every possible place. An immense craving for food jolted him upright. Before he started for home Aavi checked for any messages or missed calls. No messages but a couple of missed calls from an unknown yet familiar number, likely an adolescent customer.

A consumed bowl of steamed rice with lentils, cooked carrots and peas on spices led out a loud belch from Aavi. Food never tasted better. Aavi glanced at the black mini screen. It didn't light up, vibrate and neither was there a light blinking on the top left hand corner. He cast it aside on the sofa and slumped back on the cushions.

Why hasn't he called or texted? It's been hours. It's almost six he can't be at school teaching. Shouldn't he have assured me that everything was well there? Is he caught? Is that why there hasn't been any interaction? What will become of his wife and kid? Will they be out casted like us? Will they even survive the wrath of the deceased's parents, relatives, neighbour and angry society?

Why am I praying for his wellbeing? Surely he doesn't deserve forgiveness. A child murderer! Oh God! Couldn't he have taken up a punch bag and battered it whenever he needed to let his fury out? Who am I to talk? I was nearly there. I escaped he didn't.

What a mess!

Next day Aavi started work as early as six to make for yesterday's loss. At twenty past two he waited outside the premise of Uttampur High School. Soon a loud bell rang to conclude the day's schooling.

A continuous wave of children and adolescents in uniform stormed past the school gate. Most rushed to the ice cream vendors striking them with their voices of hunger. Patience was obviously not a topic of discussion in school. The vendors constantly had to fend their goods from the long outstretched hands and convince each face that their turn was coming and there was plenty for all. The studious and introverts left for home. The rest gathered with their friends and lingered around. Few discussed topics of whatever entertained them and few were busy communicating telepathically with the opposite gender group, staring and smiling.

Two lads aged seventeen walked up to Aavi.

"Are you booked for this evening?" said the shorter one.

"No."

"Good. I will book for today and he will for tomorrow."

"You know the drill?"

"Yeah... Be at the market place by four thirty, no delay and one hour to ourselves."

"Both of you have my number?"

"Yes."

"Good." They were about to leave when Aavi said, "Also one new rule. You all need to make a down payment."

"What?"

"Pay an advance."

"Ok...How much?"

"Half..."

They reached their wallet, took out a hundred and fifty rupees and handed it over to Aavi.

"You two are short by fifty."

"Isn't it three hundred?" The shorter one did all the talking and questioning.

"Another new rule the fee is now four hundred."

"From when...?"

"As of now..."

"You are robbing us."

"Do you want to or not?"

The indignant teenagers took out fifty rupees each. Aavi took his belongings and ordered, "Spread the fee hike and advance payment around."

Aavi sat on the edge of the broken bridge expecting to see Misty across. Alas, neither Misty's familiar shape nor any human movement was noticed. Misty had forced a communicating means and seemingly forgot of Aavi's existence. Aavi had clearly voiced his opinion of no more meeting and yet an immense desire took over him for another escapade.

Why on Earth am I moping? What am I doing? Do I really want to be associated with a criminal? Am I that lonely that I cannot see past him? Have I stooped so low to tag along with anyone that comes along the way? No. I can make another friend, I can have a friend. I have had friends before... haven't I? Huh...none.

Am I miserable or what? I should stop being so reserved and make a friend who isn't a blackmailer or a murderer. What if that someone finds out? Nahh... Misty was different. He has an advantage others don't. I'm safe.

Why hasn't he called? Uhhhhhhhhhhhh...forget him. Don't say his name, forget him. If he doesn't want to call so be it. Everything was a lie. He doesn't need a partner or me; those were necessary words to save himself. He has fooled me. First it was Mom and now he. I hate him. I hate them both.

Should I go and confess what I have done? What he has done, been doing and will continue to do so? Don't those families that have fallen mentally and physically deserve justice? Isn't their sorrow demanding enough to be wiped off? Are they fated to dwell in the past and not get closure? Don't they deserve to know the truth and say goodbye.

I can't. He might be a killer but I'm worse. So is he but he's made and sold an identity. I should have done that too. I should do it and sooner the better. Postponing shall only arouse curiosity on idle minds that have nothing better to do than to interfere, gossip and spread rumour. Irony is that their falsification couldn't have been truer.

Everything has changed. Life was mundane and simple like any others, struggles and problems, higher or lower. How life usually is. I had to complain like a greedy person. I wanted, desired and beseeched the heaven for more, an excitement and a break from this repetition. Careful what you wish for. I'm likely doomed.

What am I crying about? Nothing has happened. Be optimistic. Could I be more dramatic? I should have joined a theatre for drama. Get realistic and deal fearlessly with whatever uncertainty lies ahead.

The hour mark alarm clock ticked off. The teenager's party time was over and so was Aavi's whining.

CHAPTER SEVEN

The biggest village fair of the decade was finally here!

A rush of energy, excitement, playfulness, eagerness to doll up and feast extravagantly took over Chaanpur village. The past week was a scene of craziness. The village boomed each and every second a soul was out there on the streets. All around one could see, was a crowd gathered impatiently in front of all kinds of shops. The people of Chaanpur and all neighbouring villages alike were hell bent on filling the pockets of every possible retailer out there. It was as if they had all joined forces to take a pledge: We shall enrich every vendor out there. And surely none of those vendors were going to rant to their household of what a slow day it had been. Traffic was at its peak. Vehicles entered at a much higher ratio and forget about leaving. The roads significantly failed to accommodate any wheelers yet there was always room for one more. The whistles of the traffic police were interminable so was the infinite honking. A serious check-up for possible deafness should not be taken lightly. When people were done spending they were gossiping and conversing. Their huge paper and plastic bags of purchases didn't weigh them down. They glowed, radiated positive vibes and fed off this energy from one other. The night did come to aid for the five senses that were effortlessly strained to the maximum.

Hedges were trimmed, grasses were cut short, ground was swept, water was sprinkled to settle in the dust and stalls were cleaned and decorated. A soothing music was put on and the gates were opened.

Tia gazed all around absorbing the rainbow of colours associated with the shiny attires, twinkling jewelleries and glinting ornaments. The massive snail paced crowd astonished and bewildered her. She couldn't comprehend as to why the bigger people wouldn't let the smaller people go when it was known that all the playful things were for them. Tia usually was comfortable on her usual throne, her dad's shoulder. Not now. If she could she would have jumped, screamed to make way and run like the wind and attach herself to all that was there for the taking and only eat candies. Her eyes then spotted the Ferris wheel and immediately searched for a way on top of it. A bird flying up in the distance answered the problem. It was a puzzle for Tia as to why she couldn't fly. Her Mom and Dad always called her out 'angel' and from the numerous cartoons on TV that she devoted to watching it was clear that angels could fly. Tia was upset and angry for being tricked earlier in the evening. She should have wailed when Mom and Dad disallowed her to wear her angel outfit. Now her wings were missing and she was stuck. Tia wailed.

Shreya impulsively took Tia out of her throne and began soothing her child. She knew Tia's cry was out of impatience of waiting for so long for what they and everyone around them had gathered for. If their hearts weren't filled with excitement then the sultry climate and immobile people would have long battled out their patience and spiral them down exasperating over petty things.

From what she saw Shreya couldn't possibly conclude the delay. Tia was continuing her fits, she needed a move on to re-establish comfort and her husband stood still, unmoving, wondering, pondering and composed with an imperceptible upward curved lips.

Misty had his vision glued to his wife's after she tenderly held his hand. Their love was unmistakably depicted in the way they looked at each other. Shreya glowed in her green georgette saree. Her face matched the glow and her curls was being toyed by Tia. They both were equally beautiful and so was his love for them. Alas! It wasn't his primary reason to live.

The crowd around Misty composed of beings that made him breathe hate. He wasn't tormented or bullied during childhood. Father didn't beat him up, Mother didn't raise her voice and Teachers were neutral to him. He didn't repeat class and neither was he a standout student. What he aimed for he achieved be it average grades, descent college, post for a Mathematics teacher or marrying Shreya.

Misty had always been a thinker. As far as memory serves Misty's thought was always about the same kind of thing. Only the presentation differed. He'd come up with different ways on how the people in his line of sight could be hurt physically and the aftermath of it. An endless number of ways to figure out was exciting and practically made his day. He loathed everyone for no apparent reason and to see them bleed, cry or beg in his imaginative world was the perfect antidote. To suppress his thinking and not go cuckoo he diverted his attention to Maths.

Misty stood with his wife and kid staring at countless people, countless possibilities. Once, it had dawned on him, *what if Shreya knew what actually made him cool as a breeze in midst of a sea of smelly people? Shocked? Horrified? Terrified?* Nevertheless it would be a sad ending to that question to which she clearly wants an answer to.

Lost in people going berserk, using any available sharp objects as weapons of mass destruction, cry for attack and mercy overlapping one another Misty was bought back to reality by Tia's voice of joy. They were at the entrance and Tia not wasting a moment demanded her parents to fill her with sweetness of cotton candy.

Tia ate wildly making a mess of her face and hands. She giggled as her parents looked at her with big fake scary eyes. Shreya had the water bottle out and cleaned her angel. Plush toys were next. They were all over the games store but a few that had balloons in it too drew her attention. Misty missed the first five shots and Tia was unhappy. She wanted that panda which looked exactly like in one of her cartoons shows only not as big and then move on to uncharted territory.

Shreya took the sixth shot and the panda was Tia's followed by a rabbit, courtesy to her Dad who dislodged out all the empty paint cans resting on a woodened table with a perfect strike at the base of the two dimensional pyramid. Next Tia tossed some big rings and one of it landed on a red car. She yelled in excitement when it did land but wasn't interested at all in keeping a toy that was of no use. Her Barbie's rode in a chariot like a proper princess not cars.

A few people of her age group were running all around in groups, yelling at one another while Tia's Dad held her fingers firmly. She so wished to free her hold and whoosh away to play with the other kids. Tia's wasn't strong enough to loosen her Dad's grip and no pleading would change Dad's or Mom's mind. The last time out at a fair she ended up wasting her cries and tears.

Mickey Mouse came to her aid. A sizeable inflatable Mickey Mouse bounce house was a few metres away. Roars of laughter and giggles came from its direction. Tia put all her weight to the ground and pulled her Dad towards Mickey. Her Dad picked her up and fastened his steps.

Five families with their little devils were awaiting their turns. The parents that were in line couldn't wait for it to be over unlike those whose boys and girls were on the floor bouncing themselves to bliss. These parents had their owl's eye fixated on their offspring(s). Not for a sec did their gaze leave their precious. If they were of the notion that somehow someone would grab and flee away with their beloved they needn't worry. If it was that another kid would hurt theirs it would only be by mistake. If it was simply a habit of being careful then so be it.

A predator though loomed over them.

Time was up for the fifteen boys and girls. No more jumping. The impatient next batch rushed to Mickey's bouncy floor, pushing and shoving their exhausted counterparts whose parents yelled at this bunch of misbehaviours. Tia's elbow was sent for a shock wave by one of the bigger boy's making his escape out of the narrow gate. The sudden jolt of pain was sure to have made Tia cry out if not for the immense enthusiasm to jump and prance.

Shreya noticed the boy elbowing her daughter and half-heartedly yelled out a 'Hey!' *She'll be fine.* Like how she would be when she was little. Going out with Tia and Misty usually made Shreya sentimental. Sweet past memories overcame her present. Dearly she missed her Mom and Dad. How wonderful it would have been to connect her experience with her parents. Compare her and Tia's behaviour. Gush about similarity, laugh about nuisances. Credit the positive variance to Tia's Dad.

So much was lost for her, Tia and her parents. They would never see the reflection of their daughter in Tia. Never pass on their wisdom to their granddaughter. Give

Tia a past of grandparents love.

Her train of thoughts were interrupted by her husband.

"I need to visit the Men's room. I'll be back in ten minutes or so."

"Ok."

"Do you need to go too?"

"No I'm fine."

"Look after Tia. She will certainly want a few more rounds of it. I'll be back by then. Stay here. Don't wander around. You have money in your purse?"

"Yes."

"And your phone...?"

"Yes."

"If you do go to eat, come back here immediately. I'll be waiting here. And do not let go off Tia at all."

"You worry too much."

"Have you seen this crowd?"

"I see it and we see it every year."

"It's mammoth this year."

"It's mammoth every year." Shreya raised her eyebrows and said, "Now go before you embarrass yourself."

Kids go astray on an occasion such as this. How many? Misty didn't have the answer, five, ten or higher than ten? One at least certainly does go missing, beyond doubt. He had seen three identical white police vehicle with POLICE written on the side over a dark blue bar, parked near to the entrance. The khakis were somewhere but where? Alert? Could be? One never really can know. Sure the police station, the desks, benches, cabinets and cells plus their vehicles and clothes had lost their polish, but still, it would be foolish to assume they were not vigilant especially on an occasion such as this.

Off course, Mann's trail ceased before it could even begin. It was nothing but luck. One cannot count on it. He went beyond his process, an unwise judgement, toyed with his fear and got the better out of it. What's the guarantee for a repeat? Not every father disappeared the same day as their son unless a common person was responsible. Few whose curiosity arose were squashed by the fire Mann's father had set on their house in his drunken state. There was nothing left and no trace of the house members. It was assumed that the father left with his son for someplace else.

Ah! If only it was that elementary every time.

Once you devour a new taste it hangs loosely to be plucked again. Spending hours on the road looking for a stranded homeless brat (they are all brat) wasn't thrilling. There was no threat. The silence made Misty uneasy in the beginning. It all but became futile after he embraced the darkness and looked forward on being the predator.

In the middle of nowhere where the lights were dim and vehicles weren't passing Misty would be on the lookout for a tramp kid. Once he found his potential victim, luring them with food was an easy task. He would ask them to jump on the back seat and let him drive to their place of stay. The comfort of the car's cosy interior usually did the trick. The ones that fell for it usually slept instantly and later forever. The not so compliant one needed to be straightened out. That little hassle along with a bit of huff and puff was shut down once they were tied and locked up in the trunk. Their muffled yelling or pathetic kicking failed to attract any rescue response. Adding to their misery they weren't the kind of people that the society cared or missed. The police wasn't going to take their parents seriously, an FIR could be registered and it would be the end of the imaginary search operation. Justice isn't for everyone.

As much as this undertaking of a new route to kill enthralled Misty the motivation to replicate came for Aavi. Two weeks back, on that morning before parting ways Misty had imprinted himself in Aavi's imagination. Indisputably he had left an impression fascinating to Aavi. For how long though would Aavi drool over what had transpired?

Misty hadn't responded to Aavi's numerous calls or texts. Ignorance could lead to exasperation and in turn anger. A hot headed person is similar to a crazy bull hell bent on destroying anything and everything irrespective of the consequences. He could have simply responded and tightened that leash around Aavi. But a leash could be loosened. What Misty needed was Aavi to walk by and for him wilfully.

The circumstances were ripe and the juices needed to be devoured before left unattended to rotten state. It was critical to not miss this opportunity. Misty's grey eyes searched for its prey, any kid.

Misty had no dislike for children in particular. His bony appearance was true to what people usually perceived of him, a weakling. Overpowering a child with his feeble strength was possible. There could be no complications involved and there were none. Hence misfortune landed on their doorstep. Then there was his cowardice that directed his wrath on vagrant kids. Anyone else and there could be a search. Once a pattern develops Misty would be hunted restlessly by police and society. If he's caught, society won't be merciful. Death would bring relief to the crucifying endless pain from being beaten up by a violent mob or his prison compatriots. No one likes or forgives a child abuser or killer.

Yet he meant to pick one of these calves away from its herd and slaughter it to feel powerful.

The search began and ended as quickly. *Stupid! Stupid! Stupid!* No way could he simply walk out with a kid. He being a familiar face put him in a disadvantageous position. The one thing he didn't want was to be identified as a person seen with the missing kid. He didn't want to give away any stink to a keen nose. A suspicious mind is like a curled tail. It just doesn't straighten out.

A brat then passed by him dropping droplets from a cold orange bar on his polished black shoes. His clear reflection became hazy and Misty steps involuntarily followed the sinner. The brats to and fro motion halted Misty's pursuit. He took a stand beside a crowded game stall and kept his watch. The imp was nowhere to be seen.

Instead he saw his wandering wife and daughter obviously searching for him.

"I'm so sorry." Misty apologised immediately.

CHAPTER EIGHT

Stop running or we will SHOOT.

This is it. They will cleanse me with my blood.

Turn around with your hands behind your head.

Everyone will SEE me.

I said turn around with your hands behind your head.

I didn't do anything. I was helping the kid find his parents. You have to believe me. I'm innocent. Misty babbled.

Shut up and do as you are told.

Shreya! I'm innocent. You believe me don't you? He pleaded.

No. I don't know this stranger.

WHAT! How can you say that?

My husband doesn't kidnap little kids. You are a demon.

You heard the lady. Back off. Don't move your feet. We said don't move, freeze.

"Misty... Misty... Misty."

"Huh!" Misty snapped back to reality, his heart and head throbbing, eyes wide open he stared at Shreya.

"Are you feeling well?"

"Yeah I'm good."

Shreya questioned no further though her husband was white and pale or a series of lies would await her. He was a habitual liar and she knew it all too well. One picks up on these things in a relationship. Misty would be astonished, ashamed and mad if Shreya revealed her knowledge. She held her tongue. His lies were harmless. Whenever he did come back from his so called 'drive' Misty would be serene as to his jittery behaviour earlier. He never smelled of smoke, alcohol or women. This composed Shreya. He wasn't cheating or expending in anything, his lies were forgiven.

"I need to use the washroom." Seeing Shreya lift her eyebrows Misty said, "I'll not linger around."

A terrifying daydream had rattled Misty. It was the first time his subconscious took him to this portion of his fear. What had brought this upon him?

Misty didn't need to think twice. Aavi was at the centre of it with his queries and putting all his hard work as luck. You don't get luck by your side by sitting idly. Luck comes along with endurance. It was his efforts that took him this far. *Gosh Aavi! You may have jinxed my life.*

The stench of piss threatened a cough and Misty hurriedly finished his business and moved out of the fetid place. He led out a series of cough and took in the hot air.

The urge to carry on his act was replaced with anxiety of being caught. How was he even contemplating the idea of snatching away a kid in the middle of a well policed fair? He was supposed to bring out boldness not stupidity. How would he even manage to do the unthinkable? Shreya, Tia, friends, students and their families and above all the police and the crowd were only the few obstacles he had to overcome.

Misty was unmoving yet he felt like his whole body was convulsing. Everything and everyone seemed to be in a move or hurry. The whole world was in a swirl, dancing around him, making him sick. The plan to present a kid to Aavi was in danger. He couldn't understand how was he to carry out anything when he was being whirled.

It's a funny little world. There's always a trick up its sleeve. It takes and gives opportunity on a whim. The ice cream dropper ran past Misty once more and Misty took off.

A huge commotion broke out near the Ferris wheel. Ostensibly a woman was pinched inappropriately on her back. She let out her fury on the person behind her. The surrounding people joined in her support and gave hell to the guilty person who repeatedly pleaded his innocence and lack of knowledge of whatsoever may have occurred. A few took to his side mainly his friends and family members. The khaki people rushed to the scene and after, protracted conversations and a bit of force, successfully subjugated the crowd only after they appeased them by promising to take the clueless so adjudged guilty person into custody. He was released once they reached the police station. One look at the guy and the police knew he was innocent. They played along for the crowd to not turn the situation into a dire one.

Misty happily drove back home with his family. In one brave impulse he overcame his anxiousness and cowardice. One slight pinch turned everything in his favour. Everyone was running and yelling and amidst it he casually picked the dropper, holding the boy's head firmly against his shoulder to run past people to his car. He knocked the kid, wrapped him up in his trunk and took off to get the wife and kid.

I did it! Hehe I did it!

CHAPTER NINE

What does he think of me? A loser, who has got nothing better to do than to wait for his text at two in the night.

Aavi's face told a whole different story. Smile that kept widening, excitement that kept growing and eagerness that made him fumble things.

Wait till I meet you. That's not how you contact someone after deliberately ignoring that person. And seriously am I to disturb my sleep and follow orders from someone whom I met two weeks ago. Ha ha the guts on this guy. One punch and I could knock off all his teeth.

In a minute of that text Aavi was clothed to go. God he had been waiting, waiting and waiting. His mood swung from being vexed with Misty to giving him the benefit of doubt. Involuntarily Misty was inked to his body and he couldn't find any tools that could remove it.

"You got my text." Misty said.

Fuck you. "Seems like it, doesn't it?"

"Oh Come on. That's not a way to treat a friend."

"You are right. I shouldn't have answered or come. That's how it goes on nowadays I guess."

"I promise to make it up to you. I have a wonderful surprise waiting."

"Is that so?"

"Follow me."

Aavi followed Misty to the trunk of his car. For some reason he had forgotten who actually Misty was and he had a different kind of surprise in his mind. He was bought back to reality on seeing a kid of ten or eleven or twelve bounded by ropes that ran all across his puny body. The kid was awake. His eyes had lost hope and you could see he had been crying.

"Are you nuts?"

"Yeah..."

"Is this some kind of joke? You had agreed to keep me away from your shenanigans."

"Well I promise a lot of people a lot of things, doesn't mean anything."

"Then should I confront the police? You will be wetting your pants more than those kids. You are more of a coward than them."

"True that." Misty let the word *coward* fly past him. "Then again you are not going anywhere. You may want to but you need me alive or rather not behind bars more than you realize. I told you this before and I am telling you now. You need me more than I need you."

"I'm done with you and I don't need you."

"Are you sure you can walk away leaving this kid with me?" Aavi walked away but not far enough to be deaf to Misty's words. *Can I actually walk away?*

"Fuck the kid, are you sure you can stay away from me?" Misty shouted.

Who am I kidding? I flew away in a minute of his text like a silly fool.

"Come back you have work to do."

"I'm not doing anything."

"You are doing everything tonight."

Aavi found himself so ready to abide, oblige and be compliant to Misty, he lost trust in his reasoning. There was not an ounce of doubt that what he was doing was a certain sin and unforgiving. If there was Hell then a place was booked in advance for him. Yet here he was helping a maniac, carrying his prey to its final resting place. *You are doing everything tonight.* He had begun on a bright note.

"What did the kid do?" Aavi asked after resting the kid near about the spot he had found Misty strangling that other kid.

"Nothing significant or damning to call upon this fate yet enough for me to wrap him up... His orange bar was dripping and it found my finely polished black shoe. I had to steal him from a thousand prying eyes and I got away. Thank you God, I love you and your ways. And I even have you here. I feel so lucky." Misty was elated.

I am both lucky and unlucky. Why do you have so much baggage? Why? Answer me.

"One day you WILL be caught then what will you do?"

"Ooooooo someone's concerned." Haha... "I would kill myself before anyone gets their hands on me?"

"Are you sure you can do that? I think it will be tougher than killing these kids."

"If I don't then something much worse could happen. I wouldn't want to give the public the satisfaction of me suffering. Besides I am long way off of any police radar's"

"Someday something will go wrong and there will be no escape."

"Ahh you worry too much. I was like you in the beginning, too many negative and morality questions popping up. Once I escaped the first time, bravery came in like you wouldn't believe."

"I am not brave enough to carry on."

"It's like snapping a chicken's neck. And with your muscles it will be over even before it begins."

"That's not what I meant."

"I know." Misty raised his eyebrow. "The society's brave enough to ridicule us for being different..."

Aavi cut Misty and said," You shouldn't be talking. You have bowed to them and accepted their norms."

"I haven't bowed to them." Misty pointed at the kid and said," I am severing them."

"Yeah, by killing innocent kids..."

"Innocent! Are you kidding me? Innocent! These are the animals that will grow up and reject you and me." *I need better lines.* "Like the old saying goes better to nip a snake in the bud. No matter how much care and love you shower they are bound to bite you sooner or later." *The classic one...*

"Your kid will not or your wife. She may hate you for your betrayal but surely she will support you."

"First I am not betraying her. She is unaware of the whole truth and secondly, fuck them both." *That was cold.*

"How can you say that?"

"How can I not say? Having a kid or a wife doesn't come with compulsory sentiments. You think Shreya is going to be calm and forgiving when she finds out? And Tia, when what I am makes sense to her? The fact that I am a husband and a father is what may stop them from not turning against me or else they would be exactly like the rest of them. See here is the biggest hypocrisy of life. People only understand if they have the same problems or else they don't give a fuck? Till then they are all one and out to destroy you. Ones who are accepting they are the bigger cowards. They will not come out and fight for us. They would rather be in their comfort zone, tucked away safely and then play for both sides. For us, *what could we have done?* For others, *we have no objection. Do what you all wish.* When they will be among equals they are like, *that was so wrong what happened.* Fuck them! We don't need their sympathy. We have cauldrons of them filled by us for each other. They fail to understand that we need them by our side and not on the side." Misty was short of breath and fuming. No witty remark came to him this time.

"I agree. Still we wouldn't be any different under their situation. We are all hypocrites."

"Ohh there's no doubt about that." Misty began to laugh. "We have an advantage. We are being wronged and we can talk shit like that."

"Is this all a joke to you?"

"NO! I am trying to lighten my mood. Inside I am all steamed up. I could go and pick anyone and smash them then and there without thinking about the consequences. I cannot be that rash though. I want to continue my doings till old age. I want to wipe away as many of these scum from the face of the Earth. I want to list all my doings and slap it on people's face right before I die. I want to laugh at them from my grave. I want to make a mockery of their justice system. If we cannot get our basic rights I want to snatch away their livelihoods. The best way to hurt these people is to go after their kids. Till now I was a coward to go after the vagrant's kids. No more. With you by my side we will teach them a lesson. We will fill their world with pain so excruciating like ours that they will live like us, a statue that sees the world moving on while you are fixed at a spot cause change is never coming."

Misty took a closer step towards Aavi, laid out his hand and said, "Join me in this journey and let us spread what lonesome feels like."

"We would be uprooting lives."

"The irony... As if yours is a smooth sail."

"Please give me a way out."

"I can't. I need you. You need this, believe me."

"I want to but see I am shaking."

"Muscle it out on the kid and see the difference."

"Easy for you to say..."

"Take the first step and go with the motion. A miracle awaits you."

Aavi glanced at the kid. All the talk indirectly about his death and the kid didn't even whimper. Instead he lay cramped up under the force of the rope in a G shape, despondent. His sorry state disturbed Aavi. It could have been easier if he was a bit rebellious. *Even if I unbound him he isn't going to run.* Aavi freed him from the rope and he crouched back to his position. *It's all over and he knows.*

"I don't think I can."

Misty seeing the antics of the kid started to kick him. "Acting all tough, huh...Beg you little wimp." At first the kid clenched his teeth hard but he could hold out for so little.

"Stop it! Stop it!" Aavi cried. The kid pleaded to Aavi to help him and Aavi pushed Misty away.

"Good get that blood pumping. It was too dull to do anything anyway. Now that he's wailing like he should it should be easier."

"Decide now what you want more. Do you want to LIVE life or let live?"

"This wouldn't be living."

"How would you know if you haven't experienced it?"

Aavi lost his speech.

"Even the kid was practically hoping to be done with it. Then he saw you, your hesitation and he grabbed that opportunity. See how cleverly he manipulated you and you are out here with your Holier than thou nature. The world isn't as good and forgiving as you. You show any sign of weakness and they will hound and pounce upon you. Unmask your true self."

That's what I fear... an unmasked me.

"Too much chit-chat... Get done with and we can move on to more entertaining things."

That's what I came for.

"Now hurry."

Yep let's get on to better things. "Playing games ha," Aavi remarked on seeing his prey back to its previous position. Aavi grabbed the kid's fist and spread them wide apart while getting on top of him. *My weight alone could take his breath away.* Aavi freed the fists and took a hold of the neck. His fingers and thumb overlapped as they powerfully seized the boy's neck. Whatever yowling the boy could possibly do lasted for very few seconds. It was over even before it began for Aavi and somewhere within him he was disappointed. It wasn't anything like beating that senior black and blue and that's what he suddenly craved for and more. It was far too easy. He wanted it to last longer. *Next time...*

"I have too much energy in me and I need to let it out. You aren't talking anymore only obeying. Let's go to that car of yours." Aavi commanded.

CHAPTER TEN

Onik took his time in front of the mirror. Not to check if his hair was combed properly or admire his budding beard and moustache or if he looked alright. He was there to see right through himself. He had turned eighteen a few days ago, adulthood began. Though early stages he needed to shrug it off and move to a more grown up age. Think more deeply and observe cleverly. He needed to be proactive and considered his capabilities to do so.

It was mandatory for him to strike fear to any person dealing with him. His lean appearance was a liability to that aspect and no matter how much junk food he ate or sat his lazy ass his body was irresponsive. So he took another route, simple and exquisite. A stolen 0.22 revolver from one of his Dad's drawer always tucked to his waist. He wasn't going to win a physical fight, he knew it and the other fellow knew it. He needed an advantage and what's better than a bullet that can rip you to hell.

His life changed with his new pal. Classmates that were distant revolved around him. He was a decent looking fellow with a shock of dark hair that took the direction of the wind, lean face like the body, thin jaw, low cheekbones and grey eyes. He had the looks which unfortunately didn't bring confidence. New pal Oh Yes! The last few months being the hot property that he was he attracted the opposite sex like a neodymium magnet.

Friends and girlfriends rushed in along with teacher troubles. Once perceived as the quiet one the teachers had trouble understanding his transition to a wild animal. 'What is wrong with you?' *Nothing...* 'Why are you acting like this?' *I have always been like this.* 'Is there trouble at home?' *Mind your own business.* 'You should start behaving?' *Can't hear you...* 'This is our last warning?' *What you gonna do?* 'Don't make me raise my hand?' *Let's be honest you aren't allowed to do that.* The teachers gave up on him and endured all his misdemeanours and pranks. Onik always had a field day at school and there wasn't anyone who could do anything about it.

It was a big day for Onik. He brought changes to his life earlier this year and today a bigger change was coming. He told his reflection he was ready, come hell or heaven.

Five minutes past the last period of the day and Onik couldn't wait for school to be over. It was up to him to make it over. There was always a box of white chalk in Onik's drawer to aid him to his activities. One of his crew member's responsibilities was to see to it or else the other members took turns to slap him. The occiput of the chemistry teacher was targeted and Onik kept hitting that spot. The frequency, pace and the power behind the throw grew rapidly till the teacher walked out. The students followed, eager to savour the extra forty five minutes they had in their day.

Onik didn't leave nor his girlfriend nor his crew who stood guard out of the classroom. He did the obligatory boyfriend girlfriend small talk within ten minutes to move to first base. She was the best kisser among his past girlfriends and she always left him hanging for more. First she raised her alarm of someone walking on them so Onik put his crew on the lookout. She then allowed kissing. Onik talked about second base and she expressed her shyness. Said she wasn't comfortable with anyone close to their proximity. In a secluded area she was up for it. Today Onik couldn't take that attitude anymore. He forced his hands on her chest, she objected. His grip was tight and very uncomfortable yet she didn't dare to raise her voice. She objected trying to push him away. Her efforts left her in more pain and discomfort. Onik's dilated grey eye, messy hair and growing beard made him seem like a hungry wolf so she stopped resisting. She really liked him even before he changed his colour shade. This shade was a big sham. She saw it, discarded it and was ready to bring out the former self. Her attempts were ineffective.

Their temperature rose and Onik moved to her nether region. She let him, willingly. What could she do? She was in love and Onik had a control over her. She was eager to please, not drive him away. For too long she kept him waiting and he kept his patience. Today there was a different look to him, something that was going to take whatever it desired no matter the cost. If she resisted she sure was going to lose him forever. She couldn't do that.

They were both ready to go the distance before they came back to their senses. Surprisingly it was Onik who ceased his actions. *The bitch is right. This can't be done here.*

"Stand outside BCC and wait for me. Don't dress up and don't carry to many books. School's time over anyways, you better get going." Onik kissed her before he walked her out.

"You... Aavi..."

Aavi saw the teenager approaching. Three more to his back following him like bodyguards. It was funny to Aavi, something's never change. Past present or future there was always a gang of students who acted tough and above their age. *Silly kids...*

"What's your rate nowadays?" Onik said impertinently.

Aavi was offended. He let it slide. "500."

"That's too much. You took 300 the last time. You know we could go there by ourselves." Onik almost threatened Aavi's business.

Huh. I remember this kid! The last time he could have wet his pants at any moment. Full sleeves, hair neatly combed and down and effing polite! Now he's pulled out his shirt, rolled up his sleeve, messed his hair, got people following him and he thinks he can say any shit he wants.

"500 or no deal..."

"Ok." Onik scorned. "Pick up at the usual market place?"

"Yes. 4:30 sharp."

"Where are you off to?" Aavi asked seeing Onik and his fellows leaving. "Pay up."

"What for..?"

"What, what for? Didn't your slaves inform you about the new rule? Pay up first or else you can go there by yourself."

"Didn't you hear the guy? What are you staring at?" Onik patted the head of one of his slave with a bit of force. "Pay the money." He had only two hundred and the other two contributed the other three.

"See you pal."

I am not your pal.

Onik finally had her in a place so quiet and so far off everyone that she became the instigator of what she pushed away every time. In reality she only wanted to hold on to him so she did what she figured would please him. There was still one person who could possibly hear them, Aavi. He was off to someplace Onik had no idea about and he didn't seem like a creep who would hide behind a tree to watch two silhouettes get on. She too was aware and didn't like it one bit that there was a possibility of a person lurking to see or listen.

"Wait," said Onik. He couldn't get through it. He didn't like her and she was head over heels for him. It would be all kinds of wrong. "I can't do it." He got up and started to dress.

"Let's go for a walk. I want to show you something." Onik ordered.

Onik walked hand in hand with her and led her to the abandoned bridge.

"Did you know the mid-section of this bridge had collapsed shortly after its grand opening?"

"No."

"It was supposed to make our life easier, the fastest route from here to Chaanpur. It was going to save an hour of car ride. Stupid bridge collapsed and stupid old men that were against it from the very beginning took it as a bad omen and influenced both sides to never ever let the reconstruction begin. Even the river that ran below has almost dried up. It's mostly all sand and stone."

She didn't know what to say so she let out a Huh.

"Those old people also spread a rumour that anyone who even so steps on this bridge would be cursed and are fated to be doomed. How silly is that?"

"Yeah real silly..."

"Do you want to step and run on it with me?"

She took off without replying and he followed.

On her attempt to outrun Onik she forgot about the broken bridge. When she reached the edge her steps didn't slow. Onik grabbed her hand timely enough to pull her back. She met him face to face as her heart raced away and he kissed her. It was a long passionate kiss and she didn't want it to end.

"Hey! You alright..?"

"Hmm..." She pursued another kiss and he responded. She wasn't ready to let go but a booming cry for help shook her and she bit Onik's lip. Holding Onik's shoulder she turned her head to detect the cause of that terrible cry. Everything was a blur and she squinted to make out what was happening. When it dawned on her she let out a horrible shriek.

Onik could make out three of them, two tall and one short running around. The taller ones were trying to catch the little one. Her cry made them all stop and definitely drew their attention towards them. What was happening was unclear. Though Onik knew it wasn't anything good or anything that invited witness.

HELP ME! HELP ME! HELP ME! Echoed...

CHAPTER ELEVEN

"You ready. Quiet a fight and mouth on this one."

"Yeah... Open the trunk."

"Here goes nothing. Ta-daa...!"

The thirteen year old sprang out and made his way through the gap between his perpetrators.

"And the wretched thing is off." Aavi and Misty shared a smile and started their hunt.

Three months, four kills, fifth on the way, several nights of togetherness and Aavi formed an inseparable bond with Misty. No more doubts or guilty conscience. Like Misty foretold the first step is the hardest. Everything after that falls naturally and it did. Aavi didn't realize he had so much anger and hatred buried for everyone around him. The killing nights were so far the best. He let his rage out first on the kids and then turned savage with Misty. Misty went home with bruises. He never stopped Aavi and never complained. Aavi didn't think about it and was happy. Life was good.

Tonight they decided to not tie their prey. It was going to be a thrilling new experience. Misty was hell bent on it and finally had Aavi over the line. The kid was stubborn. On a continuous note he banged the trunk and cried for aid on top of his voice. People were still on the road and it would be foolish to assume that none heard the kid's trembling voice. Misty drove and laughed like an untamed beast. Turns were taken rashly and pot holes were ignored sending the car into frenzy. The kid sure got hit by the metal a lot and only on those times he kept his gob shut. Misty couldn't wait to show Aavi what a rascal he had fetched for them to slaughter.

Aavi caught up to the kid but the kid slipped near the slope. Tumbling down he went to the rocks and sand till he hit some part of himself with a stone. He led out a sharp cry. He somehow got up and ran when Aavi and Misty were almost to the foot of his fall. He wasn't going to outrun them especially in the open. His best chance was up that slope and hide on some tree-top. Then someone yelled in a similar tone as he had earlier. He searched for it and there they were. On top of the bridge close to the edge, two figures stood.

Misty and Aavi's steps ceased too. Misty couldn't believe their luck. One time they decide to have some adventure and unwanted spectators show up.

"Shit! I forgot we were going to set the kid loose. Those up there are probably my teenage customers."

During their last exploit Misty came up with an idea. He requested Aavi to bring his customers at the night of their kill. Aavi sensibly told him of how stupid it would be to do that. Misty agreed to disagree, he didn't care. He wanted to see how they dealt with the possible pressure of being caught. Aavi foolishly said yes and then it happened. They were hunting someone knowing that few metres away there were two teenagers. Of course they were going to tape the mouth of the kid. Bravery hadn't been instilled that far in their vein. The excitement and rush of it made them loose their senses.

Misty stood. Aavi Stood. The kid stood.

A miracle happened.

The figure that was behind pushed the figure in front. A shrill cry of NO before a loud THUD followed.

"Holy Fuck...!" Misty exclaimed.

While Misty and the kid were in awe of how their luck panned out Aavi took the opportunity to get hold of the kid and snap his neck.

"Aavi I know you are out there. I won't tell if you don't." Aavi recognized that teenager's voice and before he could respond Misty responded," We won't." *Whoever it is I like him.*

"Wow! Who knew while we were doing our business you were off to killing people...KIDS! And we thought we were doing something illegal."

"It wasn't always like that." Aavi didn't know why he had to explain anything.

"Whatever you say pal..."

I am not your pal.

"This is exciting. We kill kids you kill girls after you have slept with them. What happened there? Unable to satisfy, do they all get disappointed?" Misty wasn't taking any insult from a teenager.

"Ha... nice... ganging up. Matter of fact I didn't sleep with her and neither killed anyone before. I saved your asses is what I did. She saw you two. Obviously she would have not recognized you but Aavi...she would have figured that out. And believe me she would have informed the police or someone. And your hideout would be discovered. How many kids have you buried out here? I'm sure the police and villagers would like to know."

Onik had them. Killing him would raise more questions on Aavi and he sure wouldn't get away with it.

"I could easily spread a rumour that the girl left or she never did get on the rickshaw. My boys will back me. One thing we need to do is bring her backpack and bury it along with her or burn it or whatever. I am sure you two are the expert on this matter. How many have you killed? Five, ten...twenty...?"

"None of your business," said Misty. "We bury her they come searching for her. We let her body be discovered elsewhere, a probe into her murder is most likely to start. Are you telling the truth you haven't slept with her?"

"I swear by my Mama."

"Good. We don't need any added headache."

"We can't let her be discovered," said Aavi.

"I know dear. Missing persons are harder to find than a dead body in public display. We bury her for sure. Let those police retards sniff her out. If they can't do it within a week they will lose interest. Problem is the parents. What can you tell about them?"

"No worries there. They are separated. She's been living here with her Dad as far as I can remember. No one takes him seriously."

"We also need to rub her scent off. Aavi you take off and clean that auto of yours in ways never done before."

"If I take off who's going to take him home."

"Hmm Ok let's take care of her, hurry."

There was blood all around her head. Her arms crooked and her legs twisted. She could have been in a horror movie playing the ghost. This was too messy and Misty didn't like it. From being a lone wolf to having two people discover his doings wasn't his ideal plan. Aavi was fine but this teen wasn't. Something was off about him. No stranger kills someone to save murderers of children. Now he wasn't only helping to cover it up. Lie about her whereabouts and discover where they bury their kills. It was like a new kid in a crime organization moving too fast up the ladder only to later find out that kid was with the police. *He will destroy us.*

"You what's your name?"

"Onik..."

"Go and fetch that backpack." Onik went.

"Can we trust this kid?"

"Nope, I hate him." Aavi replied.

"I don't like him either."

"I know it's foolish but I would enjoy taking the life out of him."

"You are pissed."

"You have no idea. You know how there some people that somehow gets on your nerve."

"Hmm..."

"This kid does it for me."

"We can't let this kid's involvement go any further. When he comes back I will tell you to put her and her belongings to grave. You go and do it somewhere far away from our spot while we will clean here."

"I agree. Not so sure he will keep quiet. He's an intruder. We have to kill him. If not tonight I say we do it some other time. We must though."

"Let's not sail that far off right now. You better keep watch on her Dad. Let things settle and then we will see about...Onik."

"I have a feeling it's a mistake to let this kid walk away."

"It would be a bigger mistake to end him. His friends know you took them here. You would be the first and the last man they charge and hang for murder. We have no other option. Keep a watch on him too."

"Sure, fucking kid. Do you think it's a coincidence or he planned on being out here?"

"How the hell would I know? I only met him. You are the one giving him rides."

"What's got you flamed up?"

"Nothing... Sorry. Let's get it over with."

CHAPTER TWELVE

"I have never seen you around. Where do you live?" asked Onik after Aavi took off with the deformed dead body of his girlfriend.

"None of your business..."

"How do you know Aavi?"

"Stop the questions and clean."

"I think we are way past not knowing about each other. Wouldn't you like to know more about me? A stranger deep inside your cave of secrets..."

"Fine... Speak." Misty was annoyed.

"What do you want to know?"

"Where do you live?"

"Ha right to my whereabouts. No point in lying. You can easily find out. Do you know the market place?"

"Yeah..."

"The street right before the end of it...?"

"Hmm..."

"Yeah you walk past a few buildings and you will come across a house with a beautiful garden area. That's my home."

"Ok. What does your Dad do?"

"He manages all the labourers. You know any kind of work that needs labour force he sends them."

Fuck...his Dad could be a thug!

"Don't stress about my Dad. He won't interfere in my matter if we don't in his. You could kill me and he would still find my fault in it. That's how cool he is!" Onik's voice became heavy.

Misty gave him a pat on the back and said, "I and Aavi used to go to school together. After school I shifted to Chaanpur and I still live there."

"What do you do?"

"I'm a teacher."

Onik burst out in laughter.

"What's so funny?"

"I don't know, you being a teacher and killing your students."

"I don't and these kids are usually like stray dogs. I find them on the street, pretend to care and then now you know."

"That kid looked like he had an owner, well fed and descent enough clothes."

"Yeah I'm expanding my business."

"Now that you have Aavi by your side I guess."

The kid's smart. "Exactly..."

"Did he catch you?" Onik then answered his own question, "Obviously he caught you. He's always bringing us here. He may also come alone. One night he may have and you may have and that's it, isn't it?"

"Yeah..."

"How did you convince him to join? I don't think he has any friends. Were you two friends in school?"

"Yeah we were. I suppose he didn't want to see me in jail."

"Nah you're lying. I won't force you to tell me. It doesn't matter. He's on the team and that's more than enough."

"We aren't a team. After tonight you are on your own and don't bother us."

"Nope... I'm joining whether you like it or not."

"This isn't a social service where you can just roll in."

"It's a social service if we are getting rid of vermin like these."

"Not the girl you shoved off from the bridge."

"Unfortunate circumstances...To make a better place sometimes good people do get hurt. They don't understand. Everyone is about giving a chance. What chance? You do wrong you pay for it."

"Right... I am starting to like you."

"I knew you would."

"Don't get cocky. And let's not waste more time. Too much talking and no work makes Jack a dull boy."

"I'm not feeling up to it. Let's relax and let her blood be there or here, who the f cares?"

"I do."

"You're too cautious and see where it has led you? Two unknown people discovering your good deeds...Break loose. Let those stains remain or let nature take care of it. If we are to be caught we will no matter what the f we do. Leave it and let's have fun."

"I can't. It will give me sleepless nights."

"Stop caring about being found out. Loosen up. What good could it possibly do to you by worrying?"

"I know that. Easier said than done..."

"Only way to get past it is to start right now. I'm not cleaning anymore."

"You hardly did anything."

"And I'm not doing even that much and you should too." Onik lay back on the rough surface.

"It's not the time to joke. Get up and work."

"I stand by my words."

"Do as you wish. Teams aren't supposed to do so though."

"Ah...ha we ARE a team then. And as a team member I propose we be careless, irresponsible, rash and do whatever the f we want whenever and however to whomever. Pick up any person we want or better anyone that did us wrong and straighten him out. Put them something so horrible to face with that they wish death was the easier option. No more kids and girls. ONLY effing MEN...!"

"That does sound enticing." *This kid has spoken my heart out. How many times did I ask Aavi, plead to him. Can we two skinny men pull it off though? Catch a bigger fish?*

"I am sure if we went on our way to catch those bastards Aavi would have no choice. He will help you, if not me. Also, Aavi might as well have a person in mind whom he would like to see suffer in the worst possible way."

Oh He surely does, jackpot!

"Are you sure though you want in? Pushing someone is nothing compared to what we will do. Blood and sometimes pee both flows out. The wailing and pleading is sometimes even worse than those."

"Sounds fun..."

"Aavi's not going to like this."

"Why care so much? And don't say he's a friend."

"I need him, we would need him."

"Somehow you have him on a leash and he doesn't even know it. Smart."

"Talk softly. It's dead silent and he could hear." Misty panicked a bit.

"You fear him don't you?"

Misty nodded.

"Don't." Onik pulled out his revolver. He was shaking from within the whole time. He had his gun tucked to his pant and he knew he could count on it if anything went south.

Misty's eyes widened.

"See no need to fear anyone. One shot and even a giant comes crumbling down."

"Where did you get this?"

"I stole it."

"Were you going to use it on us?"

"If you two had decided to come after me."

"Have you ever used it on anyone?"

"Not yet. When the time comes I will and without hesitation. I don't want to die."

"Can I hold it? I have never seen or held a gun."

"Here... it's a 0.22 revolver and I know nothing else. Be careful it's loaded." Onik passed his treasured treasure to Misty.

It was chilly and the iron felt colder. Misty felt it, ran his finger across its body. He felt alive and powerful. *One shot and everything gets dark. What a safe thing to carry.*

"Isn't it a beauty?"

"Oh! Magnificent! With this no one can dare to mess with me."

"That's why I carry it all the time. Not many can boast of having one and thus the others fall in line. No more being scared of people twice or thrice your size. They only have muscle power. Their end will come even before they think of moving their limbs, only if we have to have the mettle to pull the trigger."

"I'm surely pulling the trigger if anyone comes after me. I don't want to die."

"Me too...and another thing, you cannot tell Aavi about it."

"I wasn't going to. He will run off. He will not rat us out but he will not join us in our expedition."

"Good. We do need him."

Misty gave Onik his gun and Onik hid it back.

"Are all your kills from Chaanpur?"

"Yes."

"I have another proposal. From now on I and Aavi will pick the targets once you convince him. Easier for us as we are WE and you would be too alone to capture a bigger prey. No offence."

"None taken... I even like it. For far too long I have risked everything, it's time for me to relax and enjoy the dessert directly. As for Aavi, I think I can be pretty convincing to him."

"Nice." *I did well.*

Huh! The kids smart. I like him. Still better be careful.

CHAPTER THIRTEEN

"What's wrong with you two?" Aavi was stunned on seeing Misty and Onik lying with no work done.

"Nothing" Misty said.

"I was out there doing the hardest part of the job, sweating like a pig while you two jackasses are sitting around and laughing like a hyena, so loud that I could hear you afar." Aavi was enraged at Misty. He started hating Onik even more.

"Relax Aavi. Onik made some great points."

"Yeah like what? Be a jerk and don't do anything. Let everything out in the open. Why don't we start killing in the middle of the street? I'm sure people will turn a blind eye."

"Calm down. No one ever comes here. The problem is the people on your side of the village, first you and now Onik."

"Now I am the problem."

"Stop fighting like a couple." Onik interfered.

"We are not a couple, we are a team." Misty said.

"You better keep that mouth of your shut." Aavi warned Onik and then said to Misty, "And NO, there's no team."

"We are a team and there's no escaping that. Onik's with us whether you like it or not."

"I don't like him and I don't trust him."

"That hurts," said Onik while gesturing being stabbed with a fake knife in the heart.

"I don't care."

"I was joking you dumbass. I don't give a f of what you think."

"Quiet the both of you. Behaving like children. If we are to move forward it has to be as a team and that's final. If you two cannot accept that then go on your separate ways. I was doing fine before you two clowns showed up. If I wanted to be around so much yapping I would have let the kids stay alive. One more word from either of you and I am walking out. It's not like you two will be missed. And before you two even think of ratting me out, I will take you two along with me to the hellhole and that's a promise." Misty's speech stopped Aavi from doing something rash.

Aavi's temper was still on his temples. He looked and heard Misty with quite disbelief. How could Misty not see that Onik's the one at fault here and not him? Misty's action was a betrayal. He quelled his urge to speak back despite feeling shamed by him. Onik's presence didn't affect it. It would have been the same. His response would only be damaging to both of them. He turned and walked to the insignificant stream of water that ran past this so called river. Without warning he stripped of his dusty clothes and gave them a good jerk. The cold slashed his exposed skin and Aavi like adding salt to a wounded area put water all over his body. Though Misty had his back towards him, Aavi felt his stare. He could have gone there and be out in the open for Onik to see them. The regret would be much larger than the liberty. He didn't risk it. When no droplets of water dripped from his skin he wore back his clothes and sat beside Misty viewing nature around them. His hand secretly held Misty's, away from Onik's vision and their lips took an upward curve.

Aavi didn't sleep well. Onik was on his mind. There was a natural dislike towards him and after last night it evolved into something much darker. Onik's whole show yesterday wasn't a coincidence. Upon entering the market place last night to drop Onik, Aavi's gut clenched when he halted *Otto* at Onik's residence or rather Shaanu's home. The prick had a sly smile on him as he bid adieu. The only good thing about that ride was that there was total silence. Onik didn't even attempt to talk, probably shaken by what happened thought Aavi and Aavi was never going to be in the mood to have any sort of conversation with Onik.

The ride to his home though was stressful. All he could think of was Onik and his Dad. Shaanu was bad news. His son tagging along with him and Misty was a suicidal run. Onik was interfering no matter what and he had rubbed off his charm on Misty. Misty was on his side and his Mom on Shaanu's side. This Dad Son duo was going to end him, his friend and his Mom.

The million dollar question was *Did Onik discover his Dad's adultery with his Mom?* Onik ought to be incensed if he did. Aavi couldn't find it in his heart to give his Mom a pass for this stupid...stupid relationship. Only upside was that her other clientele were off the list and she looked happier. Despite that, Aavi maintained his cold attitude towards his mother and she did not press him to be cordial.

Placing himself in Onik's shoes Aavi would have detested his dad and would have wanted to hurt him or something. Unlikely he could have done anything to him with him still being his dad and would have looked to punish someone else. Who better than the witch ruining their lives or her children?

Aavi remembered Onik and his changed outlook between the first time he met him and yesterday. There was a drastic difference, disciplined to an arrogant. It only convinced him, Onik *knew!*

CHAPTER FOURTEEN

"Hey!"

How do I face him?

"Pretty wild ha last week?"

"Not here."

"Ya let's go back, I have texted Misty to come too." Onik was excited.

"I don't think he will."

"He will." Onik took out his cell phone and showed Aavi Misty's reply 'Give me an hour or two and I will be there.'

He listened to HIM! I begged him multiple times. BEGGED! Excuse after excuse. 'No way in broad daylight. I have classes to teach. I have to go back home. Drishiti may get suspicious. People know me. They may ask too many questions.' All of it was reasonable, Aavi understood. Not now. The guilt that was heavy as a rock vanished and Onik was again on his bad side.

"No followers today?" The soft tone was gone and the resentment was back.

"O they needn't be involved in everything. Some things should stay only among friends."

"You assume too much you know, friends, pal. Take a hint of how people behave."

"I do. You aren't angry with me. It's Misty. I am not the one meddling between you two. I am making friends and if he doesn't respond or listen to you, that's on him. I haven't told him to do so. I want us to be together."

Onik was right and Aavi didn't want this conversation to go on. "Get in. You will attract attention."

Keep your friends close and enemies closer. That's what ran through Aavi's brain circuits on the ride to the abandoned bridge. Onik kept to himself and Aavi decided it was of no use to push Onik away. He was sticking to them like a rat stuck on a glue pad. Only way they were getting out was by ripping up their own flesh. He wasn't sure what Onik's motive was or whether there was even one. Onik though, acted arrogantly and yet was friendly if that makes any sense. He killed the only witness that could have identified him and associated himself with murder and murderers of children. He was saved by Onik and there was no changing that fact. He and Misty were now in his debt.

Once under the shed of the banyan tree, Onik said, "It's so cold out here, should have worn my jacket."

"No need to make small talk. Get to the point."

"You are super friendly you know. I bet you have lots of friends."

"More than you and those retards revolving around you are not your friends. I suppose you know that."

"I'm aware and I don't care. I have them by the hook and they aren't slipping away."

"Sooner or later they will and then all that arrogance you have going on will disappear as well."

"I knew you have a soft spot for me, already giving me advice like a real friend."

"I'm not. I'm stating a fact."

"Spoken like a true friend." Onik patted Aavi's shoulder.

"Touch me once more and I will break all your finger bones."

"And he's back ladies and gentlemen."

"There's no one here."

"It's a figure of speech." *You dumb fuck.* Onik headed for the bridge.

"What?" Aavi followed.

"Ahh leave it. You really need to break free you know. Talk and laugh like normal people do, make some unwise friends and fool around."

"I already have Misty."

"You do but is he there all the time? NO. Make a new friend, like me."

"No thanks."

"This is the exact attitude why you are where you are. If only you would have hung out with someone else from the beginning you wouldn't have been in this mess."

"Are you trying to separate me and Misty?"

"No. I assume no one purposely befriends a killer."

"Look at you. Your words contradict your doings."

"Oh I forgot." Hahaha... "Who am I kidding? This is the most exciting thing to happen in my life, our lives. I can't wait for our first kill."

"Isn't your dad going to find out?"

"He doesn't care."

"What if he does? You aren't going to impress him you know by killing kids."

"We are done with that. Misty and I talked. We are moving to bigger targets, MEN!"

"No, not going to happen, too risky."

"We are already at risk. If you think otherwise you are living in denial. We are going to be caught. It's a matter of when."

"That doesn't mean I will gift wrap my capture."

They took the path down to their land of killing and Misty was there waiting for them.

"Nice of you to show up," said Aavi.

"Don't pull my leg."

"Aavi's afraid to hunt MEN." Onik interrupted.

"I'm not, it's foolish."

"It's cowardice to kill kids."

"It's cowardice to push someone from the back."

"Again stop you two. You are like an old married couple. Anymore of this ever again and I am walking away forever."

Aavi gave a nod. He wasn't going to drive Misty away even if it meant to be 'friendly' to Onik.

"I got no problem with him or you." Onik defended himself.

"I don't care, just behave." Misty turned to Aavi and said, "I know we aren't in agreement about this but I need you to trust me like before. I promise...you will thank me soon."

Aavi nodded again. He didn't want to voice himself else all the wrong things would be spoken and it would get ugly. He may walk away without physical wound nevertheless he would be the one with the deepest scar. Misty gave him an assured look of their future actions and he did trust him. Life was better with him even though a thorn had come between them whose sudden sharp cuts would still be bearable with Misty on his side.

Misty had planned their further proceedings and explained it to his recruits.

CHAPTER FIFTEEN

Onik was bored. He literally wished death to himself. Even that would have been more fun than squatting behind the thick bushes waiting for a lone rider to take a leak. Three of them showed potential but they were far enough from him, Misty and Aavi to return safe to their vehicles. The only thing keeping him alert was the constant cold breeze. It attacked from all directions and he cursed himself for not wearing anything woollen. He was shivering yet his companions didn't blink an eye. He wasn't going to complain either and seem like a weakling. He had a task ahead of him and he was achieving it by any means necessary.

Misty was exhausted too. He was tired of being disciplined. He reminisced about what he had done a month after meeting Aavi. He had been wandering in his car searching for anyone with a few yards away from their parents. He had a determination about him that surprised him and was ready to pounce on any microscopic opportunity. Then there was this fourteen or fifteen years old, as fairly as Misty could guess, walking a lot ahead of his parents. The couple called his name and he turned around waiting for them to close the distance. There were few people on the street and all a good yards away from the kid. Misty rushed his car near the kid, covered his face with a handkerchief, unlocked the trunk, grabbed the kid, took a hard elbow jab on his face, shoved the kid in the trunk with great difficulty, banged it hard on the kid before closing it and took off. It took so much time that the parents reached the driver's window yelling and crying for help. Pedestrians, shopkeepers and loiterers were either too stupid to notice a crime or were of the assumption that Misty carried a weapon or were dumbstruck. Anyways it all went in Misty's favour and he couldn't stop laughing like a lunatic. The thrill of getting away was so gigantic that he had to let it out. His heart was beating like a base drum. His hands lost its poise, his legs were trembling and his back was soaking wet. *I got away.*

Aavi loved this waiting game. This was like actual hunting, only without guns and animals. There was the added danger of being caught. It was exciting, a marvellous test of mettle and sangfroid. The weather played its own part in trying to demolish their grit. This was pleasure intensified. He sincerely owed Misty a great gratitude in bringing him to this world that was clearly a part of him he didn't know existed and today especially with this new adventure that he unpleasantly ignored earlier. *Fuck being kind and fuck being careful.* Onik was right too. What were they thinking of feasting on scraps? It always left him longing for more and Misty took the fall for his unfinished desire. He was disgusted by this behaviour now that it dawned on him and felt closer to Misty who not once uttered a word or showed any sign of dissent. If anything, he at least could get along with Onik for Misty. *How bad could it be?*

It was now dark enough for even a passer-by to be oblivious that a kidnapping was taking place a few steps away from him/her. Misty relayed this information to his friends and they agreed that any single person to pull away from his vehicle would be their target. All three were now in high alert.

A vehicle did stop long after their readiness. Its headlight lit up the road ahead. The person was two feet away from Misty and to his right. Aavi was on Misty's left and Onik on Aavi's left. As stream of fluid watered the moist leaves Onik like a rabbit hurried to the person's car. The person did think he saw a figure move. He turned and saw no one. Satisfactorily he continued. Once the hiss stopped Onik turned off the headlights. The person was startled and before he could spot the reason for the darkness Misty pulled his leg by the ankles. He fell, hit his head and before he could let out a scream Aavi had raced to muffle his voice. Aavi's big strong hands covered his mouth. Onik came out as hurriedly as he went and kicked the person's private. It only led to more pain and groaning and the person somehow managed to bite Aavi's palm. Aavi applied more pressure while simultaneously giving a displeased stare to Onik who immediately ceased his activity and joined Misty in withholding the person's flailing legs. Once his body movement was subjugated Aavi freed the person's mouth and hit him hard on the face.

"Any more screams and I will beat you to death right now. We only want your car and will dump you out somewhere else. Come with us in cooperation or else you will sincerely regret it." Aavi threatened.

The person nodded to give his consent. The punch was too strong and he was too scared to moan or ramble. Misty loosened his grip and went for the person's car. Onik and Aavi released him too and he quietly followed Onik to Aavi's *Otto*. They had parked it a few meters away from the road behind a wide enough tree. Aavi followed the person in case he went brave enough to try and run.

It wasn't as difficult as they expected it to be. Only thing needed was patience, a hell lot of it.

Aavi and Onik were both surprised that their prey didn't even attempt to escape or cry for help. He rode with them to the abandoned place and sat quietly like an obedient student. Onik looked at him and tried to read his face. All he saw was an exhausted person resembling someone he couldn't recall. Misty followed them with the person's car.

"Get out," said Aavi.

"It's too cold here. I will die if you leave me here."

"You won't."

"If you say so..."

"You are one weird fellow," said Onik. He couldn't resist saying it.

"What can I do? If I don't obey you are going to kill me."

Yeah that's right you IDIOT, we will kill you. A sinister smile covered Onik's face. He was finally going to torture someone to death.

Misty meanwhile picked up a log and smashed the back of the fool's head. He fell to the ground and cried in anguish. Before he could even process his pain Onik kicked and stomped him anywhere his foot could land. Onik had never ever even patted or slapped anyone besides the shove that ended his girlfriend's life. This was an altogether new territory of experience and feelings. He enjoyed kicking aimlessly. Too many times he had wondered what if he got into a fight. He sure wasn't going to be victorious. He was extra sure that he would be the one taking all the blows and that wouldn't be pretty for him. Now he was confident that this person wasn't fighting back which gave him all the liberty he needed to execute whatever came at the spur of this moment. So he kicked, stomped and smashed the person's face with the dirty sole of his shoes.

Aavi and Misty let Onik have his fun and when he seemed done, which did take a fair amount of time, they each took a hand and dragged the person to their killing spot. That drag alone caused a fair damage to the person's body especially when a nail which had been stubbornly rooted to the ground found the person's back. The nail stung and caught his flesh. The forcible drag made sure that the nail made a nice slash to the person's skin. He squealed for so long and loud that Onik's hair stood up. *Someone could actually hear him.*

Once they were under the shade of the abandoned bridge Misty asked, "What now?"

"I don't know," Aavi responded.

"Let's all kick him together," said Onik.

"You have done enough of it already."

"Let's cut him in parts."

"We don't have the tools and I'm not sure if we have the stomach to do that."

"I don't know what else we can do if we cannot cut him or kick him." Onik gave up.

"I have an idea. We tie him up to a tree trunk. Misty you do have ropes in your car?" Misty nodded and Aavi continued, "Once he's tied we will play a game. Mark a spot at a distance straight in line to him and from there we take turns in throwing stones at him till he's dead. Whoever strikes the most, wins."

"I'm ready. What's the prize?" Onik's whole system lit up.

"I don't disagree but do you know how long that will take? He may not even die. We will be exhausted and our arms will be in so much pain," said Misty. He was secretly very impressed of how far Aavi had come along. *My beautiful work...*

"Who's ruining the party now?" Onik expressed his dissent.

"You're right. We could be here till morning. Why not we take a few shots at him and then....let Onik kill him."

"Really...?"

"Yeah...This is our welcome gift to joining our team." Misty said.

"Now we are bonding. Let's do this." Onik's lack of hesitancy surprised both Aavi and Misty. They didn't that think he had it in him to even respond let alone agree. So without wasting time, up the slope they went with Aavi carrying their toy. Misty and Onik picked a random tree and when Aavi reached they tied their toy up. Aavi drew the line from where they would aim while Misty and Onik piled up a few stones beside it and then they began their game.

Onik went first and hit the target right at its right shoulder. "Woo!" he exclaimed.

Aavi brushed his mark and Misty hit him right on his stomach. Aavi was down by a point and the competition began.

Above the head, kneecap, thigh, foot, past the hip, past the shoulder, shin, earlobe, ear, right at the left eye, kneecap, past the cheek, hit the cheek, brushed the cheek (Onik was the one who hit and did a victory dance), gut, gut, gut, gut, gut, brushed the gut (Misty out of the game), gut, gut, gut, thigh (Onik defeated). This hitting on a specific part of the body went on till the score was in Aavi's favour. He was really pumped up and wanted to unleash this extra energy on the bruised, cut and bleeding target.

Aavi sped up towards the person and Onik yelled, "Hey! He's mine."

"Fuck off."

"You are one arrogant bastard. It was decided that I get to kill him."

"I don't care."

"Aavi you are being arrogant. We decided earlier and it stays that way. You will not touch him or else we can part ways."

"I'm sick of all these talks and threats. We are a team, don't fight, we will part ways." Aavi huffed. "Truth is without me you two are nothing and don't give me that speech 'you were doing this before me.' I will do what I want and you two are staying out of it. You don't have the balls to do anything daring anyways." Aavi stormed off.

Onik was about to pull out his shiny metal friend during Aavi's speech before Misty's eyes caught his which told him not to do it.

"Your plan ended before it could even start," Onik said. Onik and Misty had texted like lovebirds this past week and Misty took quite a shine to him.

"Doesn't matter, this will do."

"Nah I don't think so. He seemed pretty angry with you. He isn't coming back."

"Oh he is!"

"You are being overconfident."

"I'm not. We needed him to be furious and he is. That's more than enough."

"Furious cause of ME not you. O I see how that is better. He can't stay angry with you, Can he?"

"I am not so sure about that." Misty told the truth. He had a hold, a strong one and he kept exercising and stretching it. One day Aavi may realize his manipulation and it will all be over. He dreaded that day.

"You will bring him back, won't you? We need him."

"I won't. Aavi will come back to us."

"He better do or we have to think of other means to capture people."

"We have your gun or has it lost its power?"

"Ha I completely forget. Ya we don't need him. Good thing is you have me."

"Ya I'm forever grateful."

"I know you didn't mean that but I choose to ignore."

"Let's do some target practice." Misty's desire to fire the gun was beyond words. His thoughts still went back to that day when he for the first time ever saw and held a gun. Instantly it gave you a feeling of being so powerful that you wondered on whom you are going to use it: A classmate that bullied you, a teacher that was partial, a neighbour that poked around too much or a relative that was too pretentious or any random person that got to your nerves.

Onik was promised of being able to use the gun tonight. He put it off as a bluff. Now it was an unexpected but welcomed situation. To say and to do was always going to be difficult and testing. He may have put a rough and strong exterior but his interiors were always trembling simultaneously out of joy and fear. He honestly didn't know whether he was enjoying or terrified of this murderous path.

"Why not...? Only one problem I didn't bring any extra bullets."

"How many do we have?"

"Eight. Fully loaded..."

"We aim three each and last one we fire it up close."

"I bet we are going to scatter his brains out."

"Let's find out." Both Misty and Onik had a menacing look about them.

Onik went first. It was his gun so obviously he should be the one testing it first. A childish thought entered his mind. He took his stance behind the line from where he had thrown stones earlier, aimed right at the person's head and without putting much of a thought fired. BANG!

The shot made such a blaring sound that it startled and rattled both Onik and Misty. Though they were miles away from the nearest police station and it would actually be impossible for them to hear that BANG both Onik and Misty feared that they did. It took a while before the ringing in their ears stopped.

"That was awesome!" exclaimed Onik once he was fully functional, "God, what a noise. My insides were buzzing... Haha..."

"Mine too, now my turn." Misty couldn't wait anymore.

"Wait... did I hit him?"

"I don't know." Misty looked at the person and said, "Don't think so."

"I'm checking first." Onik slapped the person on finding he missed his shot.

Onik reluctantly handed his gun to Misty who by observation aimed lower, fired and grazed the person's neck. "Woooooo!" he exclaimed.

Onik missed again. Misty missed too. Onik felt better, he had a chance to win this contest. He aimed lower, closed his eyes, called out God and fired. AAhhhhhhhh the person shrieked. When Onik opened his eyes and it adjusted to the surrounding he witnessed one of his most impressive works. His shot took out the person's gut, blood was streaming out of him and the agony he heard comforted him.

"I WON!"

"Not yet."

Onik prayed again. It worked again. Misty missed again. Onik burst out in laughter.

There was still some life left in the person and Onik quickly ended that by firing up close pin point at his forehead. Misty was disappointed at being outdone by Onik. He finally holed out a bullet though on a dead person. Next time he thought he was winning the shootout battle.

"We should do this again and soon," said Onik whose nerves had finally settled. He was very happy with his last shot. He felt like a real life gangster, straight execution no bullshit yapping and threatening, one shot and dead.

"Definitely....and next time I'm winning."

"Nah next time I'm going kick your ass AGAIN. Haha..."

"I'm going to kick yours right now and very hard."

"You gotta catch me first."

"I don't need to. You mess with me and you are walking home."

"Oh Shit!"

"Yup...Ha...ha..."

"Maybe I will take the dead guy's car."

"And risk us being caught."

"It doesn't matter to me."

"Tell that to me once the police have your ass all red."

"I will not be in a position to tell, will I?" Hahaha both together...

"I'm hungry," said Onik once their laughter was settled.

"Yeah I can hear your stomach."

"I have been here all day what did you expect?"

"Better self-control."

"Too big a task, where will we eat...?"

"There's a small clean restaurant where the highway ends. Its open 24hrs we could eat there."

"Hurry then. Your treat and you aren't backing away."

"Alright..."

They marched away leaving their first bullet filled victim tied to the trunk of a tree.

CHAPTER SIXTEEN

Aavi had grown short tempered of late and the unpleasant company of Onik acted as a catalyst. It wasn't that he wasn't aware of this new trait of his or didn't want to keep it on check. There was no time to ponder. It was like a reflex action. He had no control. And he didn't care.

Sure he wasn't pleased with how he had acted out last night. There was an agreement and he broke it. He was in the wrong and it was hard to accept that. He wasn't even surprised when Misty didn't support him. He expected it, yet clung to hope. This was supposed to be their thing and Onik's involvement was ruining it. That bugger was meddling too much into their affairs.

There was a definite noise of firing a bullet. It shook him, nearly made him crash his *Otto*. It came from the place he drove away and Misty wasn't carrying any. Onik was out of the question. *Have they been caught?* Aavi turned his wheel back and then didn't. If they were, he wasn't going to reach in time to save them. A sudden selfish value for his life arose in him. He found himself not caring about Misty to that extent where he needed to put his life in harm's way. It was unexpected. He thought he would act the opposite. Was that how he was going to leave Misty? Alone, stranded? Hoping for him to at least make an effort or see him one last time. Would he do the same for him? Were they two people using each other only to fulfil their own needs even after knowing things that people usually take to their graves?

Shots were fired at intervals. Aavi took it for some other people elsewhere doing whatever. He assumed that if it were the police there would have been continuous shots at least momentarily and he hadn't heard any siren sounds. So Misty was safe and he didn't have to face him. Win, win.

His mother wasn't home and he knew exactly where she was. It bothered him at first, but now, he wasn't ruining his mood for someone who didn't listen to reason. She could do whatever and stay late forever, he wasn't concerned. All that remained between them was mere formality.

Eating cold food had become a part of his life and he didn't complain. As long as there was food to eat he was satisfied. If he started to find fault there would only be raised voices and argument. He needed to rest and only silence in the house would make it possible. He had his room door shut all the time as he didn't want to see her and motivate himself to some words.

It was past noon, grey and cold. Once again he woke up late and once again he would miss the morning rush of customers. Seven days in a row. His irresponsibility should have given him nightmares. It should have affected him but it didn't. Earning money used to be everything. There was a plan to save and live life where he didn't have to think twice before buying basic needs. All of that was in the bin. He drove around aimlessly, exhausting his daily earnings and diminishing his reserve for the extra fuel. On top of that he continued buying groceries as before, letting his ego get on the way and not asking his mom for money.

Habitually, Aavi took off to no place in particular. He had a clear mind and none of yesterday's events crossed it. He pocketed a few bucks by picking customers along his way till he decided it was time to rest. He parked in a familiar place, relaxed back and let the cold get him.

Aavi woke from his unplanned nap and the first thing he saw riled him up. That his body would behave in such a way was astonishing. Everything buried inside him fought to erupt out of him. Anything that had displeased him jogged his memory. And one such awful instance came to mind when he saw his school's principal. Though the principal was all alone, all Aavi could picture was his Mom with the principal. His Mom had been in a vulnerable state because of him. And this rotten stinking garbage misused his position. *To get rid of you would be a gift to the society. Fucking piece of shit! How dare he even think to do that? How dare he? The fucking guts!! I should have taken care of him that day. How many times has he done that? Fucking cheater! Cheating on his wife! Cheating on the society! Lying to everyone! Piece of Shit! Everyone should beat the crap out of him.*

In no time Aavi pounced on the principal, knocked him out and kidnapped him in broad grey light. There were few bystanders but they failed to see Aavi's face. Daringly he even stopped near a store and bought ropes to conduct something very evil. He was in a cruel state of mind and no one was to be spared, if they tried to stop him.

"Wake up asshole," Aavi yelled after slapping the wrinkled cheeks. The principal woke up with a feeling of dread and seeing Aavi's humungous figure almost gave him a heart attack. The first thing he said was sorry, for what he had no idea. It was too quiet and the daunting figure emitted an uneasy vibe. His head still stung from the blow and he felt drained. What could he have possibly done to this person? He had always been good to others. How could that have led to this? He was perplexed.

"Remember ME!" Aavi's voice was thunderous.

The principal was confused as to what to say. Obviously this person needed to hear 'yes' but how could he possible remember someone he didn't even recall meeting, a former student? He had over thousands of students combining the years he put in behind the school desk. It was impossible to remember them. Even someone unique or an impressionist didn't usually come to his thought.

"Of course you don't you prick. But I guess you remember fucking my Mom." Aavi became furious hearing his own words. It caused a revolt in him against his principal unlike before. *How could a principal take advantage of a student's Mom?* "You fucking prick you are supposed to guide us, not betray us." *How could you do that to me?* Aavi repeated it in his mind and elsewhere his hands had a mind of its own. They went berserk on the principal, pulling him out forcefully and banging his collar bone in the process against the steel. The voice of agony was mute to the world. Once he was out of the auto the devil like hands reddened his face instantly. It drew blood from his torn lips, broken mouth and cut cheeks. The principal felt like he would go unconscious with each blow and simultaneously he felt each blow woke him up. It was a nightmare and he was stuck. *You fucking prick!* Aavi kept screaming all the while.

When the principal finally went and woke from his unconscious state he found that one rope had its end tied to his left arm and the trunk of a tree and the other rope his right arm and the auto. He knew immediately what was about to happen and such a fear struck in him that he wished it caused a heart attack before the inevitable. He yelled and pleaded to Aavi for wronging him.

"You should apologise to my Mom you fucker not me."

"I'm sorry. Please not like this."

"Oh you deserve this and more."

The principal cried out but Aavi went back to his auto, started and drove with such acceleration that immediately he heard such a joyous cry, his nerves settled.

The weak dangling arms were dislocated as he continued his wailing. There was no way he would survive this he thought. At least it would be over. Sadly he was here, alive and in unbelievable pain. Also his capturer was surely not done with him.

Aavi was lost in this beautiful melody. He never felt so alive and good about himself. Why had he not acted upon this earlier was a mystery to him. He should have never tamed his anger. It felt right to let it out. Seeing his principal in such a sorrow state gave him immense satisfaction. He had messed up his face, arms and now he was going lower. He took out a wrench from underneath his seat and in no time was all upon the deteriorated body.

Aavi was even more violent with the tool than his fist. It was not a sight to witness. One could die only by looking at this mad man taking it out on his victim. Aavi didn't hold back or flinch. He struck everywhere, brutally and continued even when he got no response of life.

To hell with you Misty.

CHAPTER SEVENTEEN

In a span of sixteen days there was a missing daughter, her father and now the school principal. Inspector Dinaat cursed himself for not taking the gambler of a father too seriously. That's why reputation is a bad thing. No matter how objective one is, you are influenced by the subjectivity.

Dinaat knew it was only his luck that had played out and nothing else. If that kind of father had come to anyone else their situation wouldn't have been any different. How could one take someone seriously who had lied all his life? He had learnt a valuable lesson: never to ignore anyone.

If the school's ex principal wouldn't have gone missing he wouldn't have even thought to investigate the father daughter duo. He wasn't at the verge of solving the case but he had a lead. The name Aavi came up.

The sooner he would put someone behind bars the sooner the telephone would stop ringing. His superiors from across town were giving him the headache of his life. It had been only two days and they made him feel like years had gone by since this investigation began. Dinaat made a rookie mistake of telling them about the father and daughter. He should have kept his mouth shut. The local press wasn't aware or else that would have been the real trouble.

Two days ago the principals wife had come to file a complaint that her husband was taken in broad daylight.

Dinaat was shocked to hear that. Never had something like that occurred out here. It was unheard of. Rarely did people go missing and to have someone kidnapped itself was surprising, let alone in the middle of the day. People on the street saw the whole incident yet none did anything to help nor did they recognise the kidnapper. *What a useless bunch of spectators.*

The principal had a good reputation around the village. No bad blood with anyone. No debts owed, no money illegally obtained. In fact he never even raised his voice on anyone. That's how simple he is or was (was wouldn't bode well for him). He prayed for 'is'. What would someone want from the old fellow wasn't easy to figure out. No ransom calls too. Usually in this kind of situation Dinaat assumed that either it would be a simple case of blackmail or revenge. Both looked out of the equation.

Next day, Dinaat questioned the teachers at school about the so called missing daughter. The teachers all said that the girl had missed school for near about three weeks which was unlike her. Her friends hadn't seen her too and somehow none of them even searched for her at home or asked about her. No boyfriend apparently, no interest in outdoor activities. Some boys told him that they had seen her being driven in an auto by a person called Aavi. He immediately didn't like that piece of information. Grown men lurking around young adult, it was too disturbing to even think what motives these kind of people had. Dinaat immediately hurried out of the school to catch the auto driver. Unfortunately he was nowhere to be seen. The other drivers gave a brief idea about the unknown person. Non friendly, not talkative and apparently drove a lot of young people. This person, Aavi, was off duty since the girl went missing. He was in the village but not anymore around the school like he usually did. The most interesting aspect from what he learned about Aavi was his Mom. It gave him an idea as to why the principal could have been kidnapped however he couldn't establish a connection to the other two. Everyone has something to hide and if Dinaat was right, the principal wasn't a saint and could well possibly be in hell. The trouble gates had opened.

Tall, broad and muscular with an innocent face, Dinaat didn't like him from the get go. There was an auto sighting at the kidnapped scene and this guy could have easily done that. He was already suspicious about this guy and talking to him raised it. Arrogant and rude would be perfect to describe the guy. No change in facial expression on the mention of any of the three missing people. No sympathetic words too. Not even a pretentious concern. There was hatred in his eyes and he didn't even try to hide it. If only Dinaat had any concrete proof. He was itching to cuff and drag him all the way to the police station. Aavi's mother was not present and Dinaat didn't ask about her whereabouts. It would have been rude he concluded in his mind and abstained from questioning about her.

He asked around and another interesting bit of information entered his ear. Aavi's Mom Reena was doing rounds with the local thug Shaanu. This was highly unexpected and if Shaanu was involved he might need a bigger task force. If he caught Shaanu his reputation was sure to take a sky high rise and undoubtedly a promotion along with it. *Huh! Headaches could be nice too.*

CHAPTER EIGHTEEN

Aavi played it cool. Cool, cool and cool. No emotions, nothing. He didn't show any, he wasn't feeling any so pretend was out of the question. His answers were straightforward. No hesitations in his voice. Have you seen your school's ex principal? No. Did you know he was missing? No. Did you know he was kidnapped in broad daylight? Yeah word gets around. Do you know who could do it? No. How is he as a person? Good guy. (Aavi didn't think too much here...or else he was sure to break). It was difficult to maintain his composure. Talking about a person that he abhorred, evident in the manner in which he killed him.

Then there were the unanticipated questions and information. Do you know Komal? No. (He had never heard the name before). Apparently she was missing for few weeks and no one had seen her. She used to go to Uttampur High School. (It struck him that it could be the girl Onik brought along and pushed to death). She was seen getting in your auto? Lots of people get in. I don't pay attention. Do you know her Dad? If I knew I would know the girl. Then he was shown a photo of the duo and asked if he was sure he hadn't seen them? I'm sure. Her Dad was missing too and so was his car. Aavi claimed he knew absolute nothing about anything although he knew about the principal, the girl maybe but the Dad that was...could it...possibly be that guy...Oh he did get nervous from within and couldn't wait for the inspector to finish his query. Thankfully that was the last of him before he left and tried to take a peek in his mother's room. Aavi ignored it.

When the inspector left Aavi didn't feel like a six feet muscular man. His whole body was soaked within a second. He was trembling. He had only begun to start a journey of his own and it looked like the end had knocked on his doorstep.

Shit! Shit! SHIT!! I have to tell Misty.

He didn't want to but he had no choice.

We buried the daughter and possibly killed the father (what a dumb luck!) and I have dug my own grave by killing the principal. What will he think when I tell him what I have done? I have jeopardised everyone. I, not Misty or even Onik but ME! Stupid! Stupid! I have made it as if a serial killer's on loose. Shit! What... have...I... done? Stupid! Stupid! What was I thinking? What will he think? Why does it matter? He will laugh at me, at my foolishness, at my brainless behaviour, he will WIN. I couldn't have just let that Onik have his way.

How could have I been such an idiot by taking the principal in a public place? Surely someone saw me. How else did that police get to me? Not a coincidence! I drove the girl to her grave. I drove her before too. I have driven lots of young ones. This doesn't look good. None of it does. I could be branded as an abuser. I haven't done anything. Every rider knows. But they could lie, to save their boyfriends and it would be easier to blame a common man. What's my word against all of them? Meaningless and suicidal...I will be hanged. First stoned and then beaten or probably killed by the angry mob.

How am I the devil then? They are the fucking evil ones. They are. They need to be punished. Not me.

Oh I even stopped to buy ropes! Oh God! What more mistakes have I made? What was the need to even do that? It was fun. Get out of your head Aavi.

I have to call Misty, that fucker. I hate him. I have to call him. He may think I miss him, I don't. He has a wife and kid. They should not pay for his mistakes, my mistakes. He was not there for the better part of my life. The remaining ones shall go like before.

I knew it! I knew it! I knew it! That pig headed has surely done something stupid. It was necessary too. He was getting over himself, wanted to take command of my business. Two weeks and he is coming back.

Onik too shall bow before me. He will see it first-hand what it is to not trust and obey me and the consequences that follow. The kid doubted me...ME. My plans always bear fruit. These two are mere pawns of mine and both shall know who the leader is...ME.

Misty was on cloud nine. He was getting back his muscle. He was going to tame it. He let it loose and it overpowered him in every way. Aavi shouldn't have kept disrespecting him in front of Onik. On the first sign itself it made him feel inferior. It was okay (actually not... he didn't realise it) when they were alone, not in front of a third person. Misty was done being driven around by people for a long...long time. He had taken charge before he was taking charge now.

He missed Aavi, not his attitude. He was getting obstinate of late. He needed to be taught a lesson and Misty didn't have to do a thing. Aavi was a self-destructive and an impetuous person. Misty relied on Aavi to do something troublesome and his breaking voice surely suggested that.

Onik was the catalyst and the fire was ignited without breaking a sweat. Everything would be back to normal. He will lead and they will follow.

Misty and Aavi had acquired a taste of each other. This addiction was Misty's backup plan. It is difficult to be left hanging once you acquire a taste of something that sends you to the moon. He was sure Aavi would at least come back for that taste.

"I did something stupid," said Aavi once he was face to face with Misty.

AHA! "Speak." Misty said cold heartedly.

"I killed the principal of our school."

Huh! Why did he go for him? "Have you come to brag about it?"

"No."

"Then... What?"

"The police are on to me."

"Why? What makes you so special?" Misty mockingly said.

"I picked him in the middle of the day in front of his house."

"WHAT!!!" *Haha Moron.*

"Yeah I know. It was careless." Aavi was upset on letting Misty down. Why did this eat him up so much? He knew. Only he wasn't ready to say it out loud. Even after lying to himself of not caring about Misty repeatedly, it didn't become his truth.

"Careless! That's the bravest thing I heard."

Those words put a smile on Aavi's face. He tried not to but his heart overcame his mind. "You know what I did was foolish."

"Foolish, yes and brave too. Now how many times did I want to do something like that you do have a fair idea. Wait... I did that too. Only I did it at night, at an unknown place to an unknown kid and you didn't give a damn about who saw you capturing your own principal."

Aavi scratched his forehead and couldn't control his laughter. His laugh was contagious as Misty joined him.

"Oh Man, what am I going to do?" Aavi asked once they settled.

"Nothing, leave it. If that police is suspicious let him drown in it. Don't break your normal routine. He has no concrete proof or else you wouldn't be standing here. Only be careful of coming out here. If this place is discovered we are likely to be doomed."

"Easier said than done..."

"Of course, however you dug your grave you have to settle it."

"If I do get caught you need to run away with your wife and kid."

"I know. I don't want to."

"There's no other way. They are innocent."

"We will see what happens. Tell me what you did and how you did it." Misty diverted the topic.

Aavi told Misty everything truthfully.

"That's quite evil and impressive. I have always wanted to kill someone I knew. You even had an easier motive...revenge. God there must have been a different kind of adrenaline rush throughout your body at that time. "

"You have no idea." Aavi cut Misty. Aavi was mighty impressed of how much importance Misty gave him. "Every past memory towards him hit me like a heat wave and made me even angrier. If possible you could say I was high with hatred. My strength grew and everything about me felt sharper and more alive. I didn't want it to end, you know. Wish that crook could hold out his breath for a longer period of time."

"Hmm you are getting me excited with all these talks."

"I did enjoy that moment a lot. It could have been even more fun if we did it together."

"Why wait then. Let's do it."

"That guy is dead. And don't we have to cover our tracks so that the police can't find out."

"Oh there's always another guy and enough with the police. You worry too much. Did we kill the girl...NO? Could anyone have possibly seen us take her father...NO? That was some coincidence wasn't it? And as far as of your valiant and successful effort, you would have literally been behind bars if there was any credible eye witness. So there's no need to scratch our head about this. It's just a bump. You see it, approach it and drive over it leaving it exactly where it was for the rest of your life. No looking back."

"I came here only to warn you for your wife and kids," said Aavi earnestly.

"It's alright. You have become a bit hot headed of late. I didn't take anything personally. You needed some alone time to blow off that hot thing in you."

"I did blow it out."

"Ha...you blew it and blew it." Misty smiled.

"What was I thinking?" Aavi said though there was not a hint of regret in his voice.

"You weren't. Else you wouldn't have."

"I don't like that Onik."

"Our hands are tied. We have to put up with him. There is no other way. We can't get rid of him or else whatever shit he may speak about his Dad not caring about him, will not save the both of us. That guy will come for our lives in an unimaginable way. He will not only take us but everyone that we share blood with. It will be horrifying. Better to let Onik think he's one of us. It actually does us no harm. He does have some wild thoughts, nothing devastating for us. It will be fun if you want it to be. Enjoy the company and everything will be alright."

"Ok."

"We could put together some things that may implicate him too if we were ever to go down. Media is a powerful tool."

"I like that." Aavi was genuinely happy with this plan. Misty surprised him. He showed that he cared for him and not that intruder. His anger faded. He wanted to go back in time to their second meeting and the days that followed. They were sweet. It was exciting and he hadn't been truly that happy since then.

"I have a wonderful idea. It will give you immense joy Aavi. Follow me."

CHAPTER NINETEEN

Aavi's expectation was blown out of proportion. His thoughts went in only one direction when it came to experience joy with Misty. It was shameful. He needed to have more self-control. Though the place to which Misty took him, called out for him to lose control. Misty dug up something from his past that in a way led to the principal's downfall.

They were standing in front of Roy's house. The foul mouthed senior Aavi had beaten up mercilessly back during schooldays. Aavi hadn't thought about Roy in a long time, not even during his activities with the principal. He didn't hold a grudge against him. He was a misbehaved teenager like most of them are at that age. It was just words...one harsh truth...from Roy's mouth. Aavi was extremely sorry for what he had done. He had sincerely regretted his actions.

"Why did you bring me here?" asked a puzzled Aavi.

"To finish what you started."

"Who says I want to?"

"I do."

"You have misunderstood me."

"I never do."

"I'm not in the mood."

"Oh you will be. Believe me. Follow me."

Aavi couldn't comprehend Misty's unbelievable confidence. Knowing him he would be right, always a trick up his sleeves.

Roy lived in a crowded place, a shock of houses all around. Every space available was used to construct a place to live in. Aavi never felt the need to live around so many people. They always pry and always have some advice that should have been followed. It would have been infuriating to live around such a hostile environment. Aavi liked his deserted place. It wasn't completely devoid of people. What few were there, were distanced enough to not meet eye to eye on a regular basis. It was right for him.

It was late, freezing and everything was at still. Aavi's clattering teeth broke the serenity. His body shook too. He wasn't nervous. It was like his body hadn't felt the cold weather that had been running for a month and now all of a sudden it submitted to it. He folded his arms across his chest to get more warmth and moved on.

Misty knocked on the gate as there was no house bell.

"What are you doing?" Aavi didn't expect this much bravery from Misty.

"You will see."

"This is crazy." *Crazier than even what I did.*

"Calm down. You are in for a surprise."

Aavi believed Misty had lost his mind.

A shy, alluring big blue eyes woman opened the gate. She was overly and improperly dressed for such a time. Her hair was fairly done, ear rings and nose pin sparkled both golden, extra bit of powder on her cheeks and a forced smile on her face. Her chest area was clearly visible and you could see how uncomfortable her movements were.

Misty and Aavi both stepped in. Aavi recognized Roy instantly. He was seated on a corner and to the right of him was a gate probably to another room. He was unmoved, strange reaction for a person whose wife unlocks doors to unknowns in the middle of the night. Aavi's perception of Roy started to downgrade. He came in with a clear mind, no past event influencing his judgement. It was off to a shaky start and Misty's point of bringing him here would be bang on.

"How much?" asked Misty.

Roy looked up. He had lost his youth. He was about the same age as Aavi and Misty yet looked like an old bedridden man. Alcohol ruined his face and body. He looked hollow. Eyes popped out, jaw bones visible, Adam's apple poking out, clothes too big for him and veins clearly visible on his slim hands. He didn't recognize his school mates.

"Two hundred for an hour and an extra hundred for each passing hour..."

Those words spoken so casually sparked a fire within Aavi. There was no shame on this person. How could he possibly be so carefree about it?

"Any restrictions on anything..?" Misty enquired.

"Nope do anything you feel like. She won't disobey. She's been taught well and if she does, hit her as much as you like. She should learn how to please customers."

The fire hit right on Aavi's head and he was ready to pounce but Misty blocked his view, him and whispered, "Wait."

Aavi's reaction went unnoticed as far as Roy was concerned.

Misty paid Roy two hundred and was ready to march on when Roy said, "Hey! What are you doing standing at the gate. Take hold of my customers and move." His wife came hurriedly and held Misty's hand and moved slowly towards the door beside Roy.

Aavi wasn't happy about all this. What did Misty want to do? He made his point. There was no need to go inside the room? This was unnecessary and uncalled for. She didn't deserve it. She didn't deserve this living and especially with Roy. Roy needed to face judgement from his hands. What a crook he turned out to be. Aavi shouldn't have been surprised. Roy lived up to his disgraceful nature. *Wait till I get my hands on you.*

"Where are you going?" asked Roy.

"In."

"That will be extra, one person 200 and for two 500."

Misty took out the remaining dues and paid Roy who said, "If I don't charge for an extra person I will be robbed blind. Everyone will know each other, come together and go together."

Misty laughed it off while Aavi tightened his wrist and took a deep breath.

Once they were inside the room Roy's wife started undoing her clothes.

"There's no need to do that." Aavi said.

She seemed confused and stood awkwardly and still.

"Why?" Misty protested.

"What why?"

"Have you ever seen a girl's?"

"No."

"Aren't you curious?"

"You know I'm not."

"How can you be so sure?"

"I'm and don't convince me otherwise." Aavi was annoyed.

"You heard him. No need to strip." Roy's wife didn't understand a single thing about what took place. She was happy that she didn't have to do anything.

"Now what?" asked Aavi.

"Now we kill her."

She heard that perfectly and screamed for HELP!!

Roy wasn't bothered about her cry. She never understood it seemed. Always screaming and pleading. He was sick of her voice. If she was dumb it would have been better. He could have been at ease and rest in peace. He wasn't even afraid of what was happening. He didn't care about her. All he needed from her was to make money. Her noncompliance to the customers usually excited them more and this behaviour acted as a magnet as their steps were drawn back here for her filling his empty pocket.

Aavi muffled her scream at once lest her husband came in.

"Let her scream, Roy won't move an inch."

"Are you crazy?" Misty's cool attitude was getting on his nerves.

"Believe me that Roy thinks she is protesting because of you know..."

"Why take the risk?"

"Because it will be fun and it will be a joke on him when we get him after her." Misty smiled wickedly.

That idea of it being a joke on Roy gladdened Aavi. It was funny. Roy may not love his wife but he had to care. She was his money pot. They would be wiping out his source of income while he knowingly sat around doing nothing. This indeed would hurt him. It would be pleasing. Aavi let go of Roy's wife and she screamed instantly for HELP!!

Misty was right as usual. They took their time to kill her, squeezing her neck back and forth, loudly enunciating vulgar words while doing nothing of that sort. They couldn't control their laughter. It was sick and they were having the time of their life. To get away like this was extraordinary. Not even the neighbours took this as an actual murder. She kept voicing her pain and the danger to her life. It was music to their ears and a sight to see as her agony was so clearly visible on her face. She was devastated by her situation and they were overjoyed. All their murders took place in moonlight. You couldn't see anything clearly and both Aavi and Misty thought that they should do this more often, able to see their victim distinctly.

Once they were done Misty and Aavi made use of the private space for their own needs. Why not? They thought. It was always uncomfortable on the ground or in the back of their vehicle and tonight was an opportunity to enjoy the soft mattress. They took it and laughed about it.

Roy was relieved when his wife stopped her yapping. It was irritating. He was sleepy and she was making sure he wasn't going to get any. He was going to give her a lesson after those two men had their way. They sure made her fuss unlike any other customer ever. *What the devil did they do to her?* For a moment Roy's heart skipped a bit but then he heard them talking and couldn't stop laughing. They sure were something else. *Men! None are innocent.*

When the door creaked to open, Roy's short sleep was broken.

"You two took your time. Pay up for the extra hours."

"Sure. First take care of your wife. She's been weeping a lot," said Misty. "And one more thing, I have to say WOW!! Man your wife. She's something else. We have never ever been excited for such a long duration. We couldn't keep our hands off her, literally. What a treasure you have and she's all yours. We will be back every other day. Wait, can we go again? Talking about her has me fired up once more."

Roy had never heard such derogatory words from any of his client. It almost shamed him and made him feel for his wife as a wife and not a money making policy.

"Thanks." That was what Roy managed to say. *Finally she's made someone so happy that they are willing to comeback desperately.*

"You are something Man. We gave your wife...I think you understand what that means... YOUR WIFE a hell of a time and many more people that came before us that too in your presence....not exactly but you can hear I guess and here you are thanking us for it." Aavi took a jibe on Roy. It was like revenge for Roy's words to him. And God he couldn't understand why it gave him relief after what he had done right now.

"Mind your own business." Roy was starting to dislike these two guys and felt unsafe. One was thin and possessed no threat but the other one was huge and muscular.

"Oh we did by giving YOUR WIFE the fuck of a lifetime. I guess you couldn't that's why she needed so many men to shake off your smell." Aavi was on fire. Even Misty raised his eyebrows.

Roy knew it was pointless to argue. He was in no position where that would bode well for him. "Give me my money and go," said Roy politely and helplessly.

"First, check on your wife mate. We have seriously done unspeakable things to her," said Aavi. "She was something wasn't she?" Aavi questioned Misty.

"Oh! Yeah! The best we ever had."

"What resistance."

"Unlike I have ever encountered."

"And how firm was she?"

"Like a flower, delicate."

Roy ignored their talks and went on to check on his wife.

"NO...NO...NO...No...No...no...." Roy kept saying.

Aavi and Misty walked in the room.

"What have you done you monsters? She's not breathing?"

"We killed her. Wasn't that evident," said Misty.

"Why? Why? You ...you had her...for what you desired...why kill her?" Roy couldn't grasp this unfortunate event. He had not done anything to anyone and neither did his wife to deserve this. Why kill her? They could have had their way and be done with it.

"Oh we didn't fuck her. We were never interested in that or her or women," said Aavi. For the first he had spoken out loud about his desires. Roy was unveiling things in him.

Roy's state of mind was useless. He had no idea what to do. His wife was dead, his earnings gone and the killers were here and too casual as if they had a drink together.

"You don't remember me do you Roy?"

Roy drew a blank face to Aavi.

"Hehe he is the one that beat you up good in school. Remember?" said Misty enthusiastically.

Roy remembered at once. He had never been in a fight or taken a beating except that one time. It was brutal. A tremor passed through his body. It took him weeks to recover. It was painful physically and mentally. That was the last time he had ever been rude to anyone by words except his wife. He never did recover from that incident. It left him weak and useless. He was like a scrap in a junkyard. He got left alone. His friends sympathised with him, he didn't like it, he didn't have that presence he used to have and it only pushed him away. His life had changed since that incident and the man responsible was standing before him.

A sudden surge of energy emerged within Roy as he charged towards Aavi. It was futile. There was no match. It was once again shameful for him. Aavi stopped him and pushed him beside his dead wife.

"You really thought you could take him? What a foolish guy?" Misty was amazed by Roy's guts. He made the scenario even more interesting than he had anticipated.

Roy immediately went back to being helpless. That one moment of courage wasn't going to take place again. It was crushed before it even began and the place from where it arose was now intimidated and scared by the person in front.

What kind of place are we living in? A man is using his wife's body to make money instead of going out to do some actual work. "What is wrong with you?" Aavi said rather loudly than he meant to. "You are not even sorry for your dead wife. She is DEAD!! A person is dead, your WIFE and all that comes across your mind is money." Aavi's steps went near enough Roy to lay a tight slap across his face. "Your kind of people disgust me." Aavi then spat on Roy's face. "We did her a favour by killing her. She will not suffer any more on your hands, whoring out your own wife. What kind of sick person does that?"

"I told you, you wouldn't be disappointed," said Misty.

"Oh I'm very disappointed with the kind of world we are living in. The weak always gets preyed upon. Look at this piece of crap right here." Aavi gave a tight pat to Roy's head. "You think you have seen people and then here's Roy to surprise you even more." Aavi slapped Roy's cheeks once again. "What a world. What a night and what a last few days."

"Why don't we tell Roy what we been up to?"

"Yes that will cheer him up."

Misty and Aavi sat on either side of Roy. Roy jumped a bit. He was extremely scared. Two mad men had entered his house and destroyed his world. He knew they would kill him. How slowly or painfully was his biggest fear. He knew he would not be able to fight them. Only a miracle would save him and that was out of the question. His wife was screaming on top of her voice for her life. What did he do? Sat like a fool right outside her room. There was no expectancy of any sort for a neighbour to come to his aid.

"So Roy we have been killing people left and right nowadays while you have been whoring out your wife." Misty stated a fact.

WHAT! Roy exclaimed in his head but couldn't speak it out. He had lost his voice.

"Few days back we killed our principal too!" said Misty cheerfully.

Roy had heard from somewhere that their old school principal was missing or abducted something like that. He didn't care. Now he was sitting with the murderers. Probably the only person who knew for certain that the principal was dead. He didn't even doubt Misty and Aavi. They literally killed a person few moments ago.

"Do you want to know what we did?"

NO.

"See Aavi here abducted him right in front of his house in daytime. He met me in a quiet place. There we had fun scaring him first. Beat him black and blue all over with our fist. Aavi the genius he is came up with a wonderful idea. He tied the principal's right arm to a tree and the other arm to his auto. Guess what happened?"

Roy was silent. His whole body was quivering in fright.

"Let's just show him," Aavi said all of a sudden, got up and took Roy's left arm. Misty took his right. Roy wet his pants.

"No respect for the dead. Who pisses on their dead wife?" Misty questioned.

"Look at yourself Roy. How pathetic you have become? That entire attitude and confidence all lost. All you have done is tame an innocent girl. You know who does that? Cowards! You are a coward. Had it not been this way we wouldn't have ended up here. Your relentless ruthlessness towards your wife wasn't going to go unpunished. Someone had to take action. Don't you agree?"

Roy nodded without thinking. Thinking would be bad. It would take a moment to reply. His impatient customer would consider it rude. He had wet his pants without even being harmed. He knew what was going to become of him. It was inevitable. They were delaying it. It gave false hope of escape. Sitting beside a dead body restored fear.

Roy was aware that unpleasant words would be directed at him on face or behind his back for his actions. He had taken it into account before venturing into his idea and genuinely had no problems with his morality. People will always bark and have something to say. It didn't matter. He had a way to earn without putting any effort and only a fool would let an opportunity such as this slide past him. He had no shame whatsoever and he had no feelings or love for his wife. He had no regrets, had. Now he did, plenty. His decision would backfire in such a way was beyond his chain of thoughts.

This waiting and mind games from his former schoolmates was bothering Roy more than the dead corpse. He wanted all of this to be over like any other who would have been in this position. For the life of him he never thought this was how his end would come. Being murdered is bad. Knowing that you were going to be killed was frightening in a way one had to experience it first-hand. He was one of those lucky ones.

"Can you hear a fucking word that I am saying?" Aavi yelled. "Is this the time to get lost in thought?"

Roy woke from his muse and got slapped by Aavi left and right. How stupid of him to get lost in such a crucial time? Well he wanted all of this to be over. Guess his wish was going to be granted. He didn't even have the time to react to Aavi's slaps. He was receiving one after the other in quick succession.

Misty there was lost in nostalgia. Finally he could get to see what was unfinished.

Both Roy and Misty were in for disappointment as Aavi ceased his actions.

"Not so easily. I'm going to make you go through hell before I take your breath away." Aavi's words had a weight and seriousness to it. It made Roy get up and run only for him to trip on his fourth step. Both Aavi and Misty burst out in laughter.

"Looks like even the Gods want us to carry on," said Misty.

Roy lay there on the floor. He lost the energy to even get up.

"Let's start the party."

CHAPTER TWENTY

Roy behaved like an obedient student which he was so not. In truth he had given up and accepted his forthcoming pain and death. Resisting and fighting would only make it tougher on him. So when Aavi and Misty asked him to accompany them in their car to whatever place they would take him, he went politely. Their threat for him for not complying was inaudible to him. He really had no hope whatsoever. Even his would be murderers knew that. They asked him to be seated on the back seat while they carried and brought his dead wife to the trunk of their car and Roy didn't move an inch. He could have made a run for his life, one final attempt, he didn't. He relaxed his back against the leather. It felt good. His back was paining. Sitting on that chair like a watchman all night and most of the time at day had taken a toll on his back. The chair wasn't comfortable too. It was a plastic one. Not leather, not like this back seat. It would have been nice to own a leather chair. Alcohol snatched that away from him.

Once they were done, Misty and Aavi took the front seats with Misty behind the wheel. Roy was somehow happy that he was left alone in the back. He wanted to ask them how long the drive was but he didn't have it in him to speak to them. He chose to ignore his captors and ran his hand through the soft leather and slowly leaned his whole body against it. He fell asleep.

It was his last sweet and comfortable sleep. He had no dreams or nightmare. Roy felt as if he slept a solid eight hours on a twenty minute ride. He was energetic and felt like he could actually do some work. Alas! Roy woke up to his executioners who he thought had the devils smile. It was dark and he slowly adjusted to the fading moonlight. Reality of what could happen surrounded his mind and his body trembled.

They were parked under a banyan tree and he assumed it was their parking spot. He walked with them in the cold like school buddies about to take a drag and have a long chat. He didn't recognize this place like so many others who they might have brought. His legs felt heavy and it was difficult to walk for long in this weather. The sooner they reached their final destination the better.

Roy took in the surrounding of what possibly may be the last place he would see. He was under a weary broken bridge. It was a surprise to come across a bridge in the middle of nowhere especially in an unused path. He had no idea which villages or towns it would have connected and couldn't understand why it was never repaired. The water flowing under it was scarce too. Rock, sand and pebbles all over.

"Are you ready Roy?"

Misty startled him. *Ready? Was he kidding? Ready? Could anyone possibly be?*

"Yes." Roy's words surprised him. Was he?

"Good. This won't be easy on you."

I know. God ease my pain. Please!

His head rang like someone struck the bell of a temple. Not once or twice, more like a thousand times. The pain was unbearable. Roy cried out loud on top of his voice. He was on his feet which was really astonishing. Aavi had picked a stone and struck hard on the back of his head. He wasn't bleeding though the hit area was swollen. He held that area with his hands. The hit was expected. The suddenness wasn't.

Aavi pushed him to the ground. Roy was busy protecting his head. He lay flat on his back. Aavi kneeled around his stomach. Roy knew what was coming. He was gasping for air as he was being squeezed out of breath. Involuntarily he tried to take Aavi's strong and rough hands off his neck. Naturally the swollen area touched surface and he experienced more pain. It would all be over soon. NO. Aavi loosened his grasp. Roy took in the air like a starving kid takes food. Gobbled up all that he could like there was shortage and no time. Air never felt so precious.

"Not so easily," said Aavi.

Misty then had his share of fun with Roy's neck.

What more? Just get it over with.

"We should try something new. This is boring," said Misty in a serious tone.

"I agree."

"Let's chop him off to bits and pieces."

"Do you have a sharp knife or even a knife?"

"No. Shit!" Misty stomped his foot.

"That could have been fun."

"No shit, obviously. Next time I will bring a razor sharp knife."

"You better. You raised my hope and squandered it even before I could fathom. "

"Smile Roy, you just got saved."

Yeah lucky me!

CHAPTER TWENTY-ONE

"Hey!"

Misty, Aavi and Roy all searched for the source of it. Misty and Aavi knew the voice well.

"Having fun without me?" The figure was behind them and was inching closer.

"Where the hell did you come from?" Misty was genuinely surprised to see Onik. Aavi's body repulsed at the sound of Onik. Roy was confused.

"Ha you thought you could hide from me and go on your little escapades."

"That was the idea," said Misty.

"I am here now and I am joining the fun."

"Were you following us?"

"Yes."

"What?"

"No. Hahahahaha.......... Dumb luck, I was out here." Onik lied.

"Trouble at home..?"

"Don't want to talk about it."

Aavi wondered how closely Misty knew Onik.

"Get in here, more the merrier."

"What's with this Dumbo? Why is he not running away?"

"He's an old friend. Roy, Onik."

"Oh! Are we not then..... You know?"

"Of course we are killing Roy. He has lost all hope. He has accepted his fortune."

"This isn't going to be fun then." Onik was disappointed.

"We will make it fun." Aavi interrupted, "To be clear I am killing him." It was his unfinished business and he wasn't letting Onik interfere.

Misty made a gesture at Onik hinting him to keep his mouth shut. "What are we going to do with him?" asked Misty.

"That was too much work," said Aavi who was as exhausted as Misty and Onik.

"We have Onik to thank for it. Are you happy?" asked Misty who kept catching his breath.

"Don't blame me. I didn't force you two to agree. I was surprised you two went along even after that bugger refused to give up."

"He was a tough bastard." Misty stated.

"Totally worth it though," said Aavi.

"Ya..." Misty and Onik agreed.

They took a few minutes to relax before Misty spoke, "I think I might be sick with all the sweat inside and the continuous cold breeze hitting me."

"I didn't even think of that. Now I might be too," said Onik.

"We need a hot bath and warm blankets," said Aavi.

"Do we leave?" asked Onik.

"Obviously, I don't even know why we are sitting here like fools," said Misty.

"We needed to relax." Aavi gave him a reminder.

"Oh! God! My body aches, that was so tiring. Never again," said Misty.

"Never again..." Aavi agreed.

"It was awesome though, right?" Onik wanted to know that his idea was good.

"Definitely worth the effort," said Aavi. Those shrieks injected delight into his veins. Roy deserved what he got.

"No more going up and down the bridge and dragging a body from the next time we cut through a person." said Misty.

"Who's bringing the blade?" asked Onik.

"You," replied Aavi.

"Why me...?"

"Cause they may be laying around your house," said Misty.

"I don't think so," said Onik.

"You don't know what's in your house?" asked Aavi.

"As if you know everything about yours..." Onik took a jab at Aavi.

Aavi somehow didn't flare up. He was too tired with all the lifting.

"Still it would be easier for you to get them than us. I'm sure they would be in your Dad's workshop," said Misty.

"They could be. I will look. Only because I am too excited of this prospect of chopping off a person," said Onik.

"I am excited too. I won't lie. It would have been so much better if we could have done that with Roy." Aavi wondered of the thrill he could have got watching Roy's expression, forgetting that out here in the moonlight everything they saw was vague.

"That bastard actually deserved a crueller fate. He got off easy," said Misty.

"No he didn't," said Onik. His plan was beautiful and the horror it gave their victim was deeply satisfying. No one could just hint that it wasn't painful enough.

"Neither did we," said Aavi.

They all cackled in laughter.

CHAPTER TWENTY-TWO

Dinaat began tailing Reena. When he had arrived to her place she was closing the front door. Dressed extravagantly Dinaat assumed she was going to meet someone special. It was grey and getting darker yet her ears, neck and wrist gleamed golden. Her lips were curled and her face lit. A black shiny SUV was waiting for her and wherever it was about to take her and to whomever Dinaat needed to know.

He had come here to see her reaction about the accusations on her son. Whether she was aware of it or not? How much she knew about any of it? What was their bond like? If any quarrel had taken place to lead to this alleged kidnapping or murder? People usually tend to do stupid things in the wake of anger.

So far there was no trace whatsoever of the daughter, father and principal. Considering the principal was taken in broad grey light it was surprising there were no leads. These three seemed too connected to not be. Maybe one was a crime of passion and the others to shut their knowledge about it or something else.

Aavi was a very strong suspect even though no commoner could identify him as the person who kidnapped the principal. Dinaat had a profound feeling it was Aavi. He couldn't shake it off and he had to pursue till there was absolute certainty of him being right or wrong. His auto always lingered around the school's vicinity. It could be straight forward as picking customers only if the people around the market place hadn't mentioned of only seeing teenagers in his auto. One oversized person ranted about being refused to let in even though the auto was empty. That seemed odd and suspicious and only grew Dinaat's tingling radar.

The vehicle headed down a familiar path. His nerves became unsettled upon realisation. *Shaanu*...Dinaat immediately backed off. He completely forgot about it. Somehow he was expecting her to be driven to someplace else. Files with that name should have been on every stations desk, the person definitely behind bars. None existed. Nothing would have been accomplished. You take down one and another rises. Then the other needs to be pinned down. And on it goes, this endless cycle. A career where there would be more enemies than friends. A career that maybe would end even before it begins. Life or lives would be lost. Was it really worth dragging himself to death?

An adversary of this magnitude wasn't wise. He would not live nor let live if put in harm's way. Many would be in real danger. Dinaat took the easier immoral option. No regrets, no lost sleep and no nightmares. Surprisingly no dead bodies and missing person which made it easier to look the other way.

If Shaanu was anyhow involved in these disappearances Dinaat wasn't sure he could let it pass. The drunken Dad and the withered principal he could come to an agreement with himself but the teenage girl, not in any lifetime.

Dinaat was a screw up. He disrespected his wife and kid and lost them. Some days he missed his daughter. An impulse would spark to go and visit. He was a cop. If his wife thought he couldn't find her new resident she thought too less of him. He never visited. His daughter never called him or even made an attempt nor did he. The relationship was too strained. Repair was impossible. He wasn't even sorry. So an apology would be a farce.

Now he had an opportunity to do the right thing. He was not old, not even retiring age. Death was far off. Many years left to sit back and relax or go on vacations with those soiled money. He was ready to lose them all. No regrets.

Dinaat made a decision to fight for this teenager. One right thing to do, to be remembered by and maybe it would reach his daughter's ears. Something even if she ignored would somehow remain within. One good deed her Dad did.

Reena arrived after for what seemed like an eternity. The weather had worsened as Dinaat waited patiently for her to come back to her place. He was cold all over like his car. The temporary opaque windows needed constant rub from his forearm. He shivered, his teeth clattered and his legs shook violently. None broke his resolve to have the talk with Reena.

He pitied her. She was in deep trouble. No way she wasn't aware about Shaanu's activities. And if he remembered correctly that guy was married and had children. She had a smile on her face though she wasn't smiling, the kind of smile when you are happy and in love. *Oh Dear!*

What had she got herself into? It wasn't going to end well. It was not his problem.

"Reena," he called out loudly through the harsh wind.

Reena saw the police officer approaching and hurried her way through the door. She wasn't quick enough.

"You aren't in trouble."

She didn't speak.

"Can I come inside?"

She just stared at him with a blank face hoping he would run away because of her attitude.

"It's freezing. Please."

Reluctantly she agreed.

"I wanted to talk to you about Aavi," Dinaat said after gulping down three glasses of water. Reena had raised her eyes while filling the third glass. Dinaat noticed and ignored.

"Is he in trouble?"

"Yes and you can help me steer his troubles away."

Reena became attentive at once. The disgust she had for khaki people had to be put aside for her son.

"What has he done?"

"He kidnapped a person in broad daylight. You may know him. Mr Lath."

Reena's expression was an 'Oh FUCK' one. It was clear she recognized the name and the reason for it to happen.

"I assume it is true."

She couldn't get the words to come out.

"Take your time. It's not every day a Mother hears her son has kidnapped and possibly killed that someone."

"WH...A...T..?"

"My mistake I shouldn't have said that. We have not yet found Mr Lath. I assume that he is dead. We have had no ransom calls and it's been weeks since his disappearance."

Deep down Reena wasn't that shocked as she displayed her emotions. She remembered that day when Aavi caught her and Mr Lath. Somehow he channelled his anger to someplace else and didn't take any action. Yet it was bound to come out sooner or later.

Aavi never was the one to speak out. Everything he felt she could see was supressed deep within him, never sharing anything. He was alone and sad and she could never reach out to him. There was a flicker of joy in his eyes these past few months. What happened for him to snap like this?

"Why did he go after Mr Lath?"

"He caught us."

"And this happened recently?"

"No. No. Years back when he was still in school."

Dinaat at once could see what possibly could have happened. A bad day, an unwanted person on sight resurfacing the hatred buried deep down leading to stupidity.

"Do you think he can kill?"

"Yes." Reena said it instantly.

"What makes you think that? No mother usually would say that."

"He beat up a kid at school, a senior. The kid was in bad shape. He could have killed then were it not for the teacher that interfered." All her words were eating up her insides. What kind of a Mother was she to throw her only son under the bus? Where was her protective nature that was born the moment she gave birth? Had she lost her love? Did it fade away? Can it fade away?

"Has he beaten up anyone else?"

"No. That was the last. He seriously regretted his actions. I could see it on his face. He struggled and suffered for what he did within himself or else, you would have been here when he was a teenager."

Dinaat didn't correct her. He was in his early forties not sixties. He would still have been a rookie and been out in the field searching for something his boss would have ordered.

"Do you think he would harm a teenage girl?"

"What makes you say that?"

"A girl is missing and she was seen last in your son's auto."

"That's his job to pick and drop. How is it relevant?"

"You are right but he has been seen loitering around the school vicinity almost every day and has also been sighted and accused by locals of only picking up adolescents."

Reena was unaware of this but she knew her son. "Why he picks them I don't know. I have no answers. Believe me when I say he wouldn't harm them. The principal I can believe not someone else."

"I will keep that in mind. Has he made any new acquaintance or some old one that you think is capable of doing this?"

"No. He doesn't have any, never did. Always a loner, it's not weird. He is different, quiet, but a good person. Not a freak."

"I wasn't going to imply that. I don't know what else I can ask you except can I take a look at his room? Maybe I can find something?"

Reluctantly Reena granted him the permission.

Aavi's room was on the right to Dinaat, a tiny room, big enough to fit a six foot person and a wardrobe. The space was tidy, bed well-made and not a speck of dust on any surface. As expected the wardrobe was locked. There wasn't anything under the bed and nothing else left to examine. Dinaat was done here.

"It would be easy if he came forward rather than I catch him. Tell him or rather reason it out with him. It will save us all a lot of trouble."

CHAPTER TWENTY-THREE

She should have been worried, she was. She should have been frightened, she was. Yet pride prevailed. She did what she could for her son. Then again it wasn't necessary had Lath actually been a decent person. He saw an opportunity and took it. Not so wrong if read in a literal sense, although, it was all kinds of wrong. She never felt as forced as she did with Lath. He had an image and he displayed it to perfection. Behind it he was nothing but a pervert. How many like her fell to him she had no idea. She wasn't a credible person and none would believe her and even if they did they would chose to ignore or just store her accusations deep inside never to surface.

So yes, she didn't feel bad for Lath. She felt happy that he got what he deserved. Although too late but that's how usually justice is served.

Her son Aavi what was to happen to him? It's all fair and pretty to know he did it for her until those actions consequences starts knocking on your front door. He needs to be warned and escape. Dinaat was surely keeping a watch. It won't be easy. She couldn't bear to see her son behind bars. Immediately she called him. It rung, rung and rung and as usual he didn't pick up. She needed this friction between them to be over. She loved her son and he needed to know that. He obviously knows but he needs to hear it. He had always been different like his father. This world wasn't made for them. She helped her husband as much as she could. She loved him and she sacrificed everything for him only for him to be swallowed up by the river. He left his mark in her and his memories. Difficult as it was she shouldn't have failed their son. She was the grown up and should have taken proper care of Aavi. She did alright just not enough.

Shortly after, Aavi came in. He had his keys so he didn't knock or ring the bell. He saw his mother waiting and knew a dialogue was coming.

"Where were you?"

"None of your business," said Aavi rather rudely.

"You are my son and everything about you is my business." She was prepared for his harsh words and was ready to take it up her chin. No regrettable reaction this time.

"What does it matter? I'm home in one piece. I can take care of myself."

"I know that and I'm not worried about you but others."

"What do you mean?" Aavi was perplexed.

"I know about Lath."

Aavi's hair rose. *How could she know?*

"An inspector named Dinaat came looking for you."

That bastard!

"So you met him."

"Have you become a mind reader?"

"I don't need to read anything. I raised you. I know you better than you think."

"You have no idea."

"What happened to the guy you are or was seeing?"

Aavi was shocked. If his hair rose that time now it sky rocketed to the moon.

"See I know you."

"How?" asked a puzzled Aavi.

"Your father was the same."

"WHAT?"

"He was like you. I loved him anyways."

"And you were OK with that?"

"He loved me not like I did. It was enough for me. I helped him he helped me. You came and we both loved you."

"You never talk about him. You never even mention him. Is he alive?"

"I don't talk because it is painful. And you know he's dead. We wouldn't be living like this if he was alive. It's my fault I didn't tell you much about him."

"I know. I never met him yet I miss him."

"I'm sorry son." Reena's rheumy eyes didn't hold back her tears.

"I'm sorry too."

They hugged each other, the last time they did was so long ago that it felt like the first time.

For once they dined and didn't eat like strangers.

"Now tell me," said Reena after they sat down on their worn out couch.

Aavi began with why there were always teenagers in his vehicle. Reena couldn't believe, *Really Aavi?* Of course he changed the details of his first meeting with Misty. He just happened to be there near the abandoned bridge thinking about things far from the crowd. Reena noticed the spark in her son's eyes when he mentioned Misty. It truly filled her heart with joy knowing he found someone.

Then they kept meeting and one thing led to the other and like how a relation progresses, they fought. Aavi mentioned he lost his cool. The fear of losing someone forever for such a trivial matter circled his insides to an unforgiving path, wrong frame of mind, wrong person to encounter and wrong ideas taking over to doing all kinds of wrong. He left out how he actually killed Lath and Reena was spared the details of how her son took a life away. All that stupid pride she had felt a while ago seemed even more stupid.

Aavi tried to sound remorseful of what he did; his eyes told a different tale. He enjoyed it. It shook Reena. He killed someone. It was a big deal. Not every day you come to know your son's a killer. If he could kill he could lie. Lying is certainly the easier out of the two. What was he hiding? It was easy she thought. Misty. *That son of a bitch was actually the problem.* She didn't say it. It was clear she shouldn't. The bridge that was closed between them would open back. She needed to save Aavi from him.

"Does he know of what you have done?"

"NO. I can't tell him that. It would drive him away, anyone and everyone, except you it seems."

"Nothing can drive me away from you. I hope not or else I would be a terrible Mother."

They shared a laugh.

"I know it's not easy to process all this information. I have strayed along a dark path and I have put you in its midst. You are putting up a brave face and I couldn't be more thankful."

"A child doesn't need to thank their Mother. A Mother will do anything for their child. I wish we had talked more about everything. I could have saved you from all of this... "

Aavi cut her short, "I don't need anyone's saving." He immediately realised his rudeness and apologized. "I don't know why I did that. I think I'm still angry with you from within. You should be the one lashing out on me. I'm the terrible person."

"Don't say that. I haven't been around you like I should have. I knew you were different. I should have taken extra care to ease you into this cruel world. I have failed you. I should be the one who should have been more responsible."

"I have so much anger within me. I don't know what to do. I have vented it all out doing the wrong things."

Wrong things! What more have you done my son, Killed more people? For her son to not appear inhumane in her eyes Reena didn't press any further. It was better to live a life of lies than to surely know things that would give her never ending nightmares. Then again she needed to know so she asked, "Tell me honestly does Misty know?"

It was not a question. It was more of confirming what she suspected. Aavi said truthfully, "Yes."

Is he the one who instigated all of this? Is there even a doubt? My sweet son, Oh! God! Why are you so cruel? All his life he's been truly alone and you make a mockery of his situation. I hate you. She nearly said it out aloud.

Aavi could see the anger dawning on his Mom's face. "I'm sorry Mom." His cold voice betrayed his apology.

"What's done is done, Son. No need for apologies. We need to figure out how to get that cop off your back. He doesn't look like a person who will give up on chasing you, be it wherever you run off or not. He had the worst thing a cop could have, determination. That's not easily worn off." Reena's dropped shoulder tightened. She was tensed.

In reality Aavi didn't care much about being caught or facing the consequences for his actions. Now that his mother was involved it changed a few things. Some secrets should never surface, his time with Misty being one. If she knew it would obliterate her. Moreover, Misty can't find out about all of what has occurred. Also, he needed to get his mom away from all of this and especially from that crook

Shaanu. Of all the men in the world she had to fall for that guy, a bit of flare sparked within him just thinking about it. That guy was dangerous and to actually get away from him was more of a problem than the police. He was in trouble but his Mom was in a tornado. She needed his succour more than he needed hers.

"They say no body no crime. Do you think they will find Lath's remains or have you disposed of every possible part of his?" The words out of her mouth were alien and disturbing to her.

"What?" Aavi was preoccupied with a nodus called Shaanu.

Reena painfully had to repeat those horrifying words.

"He isn't going to find Lath. I took good care of it." Instantly Aavi doubted his confidence. *If they find the abandoned bridge they find a lot more than Lath, innocent, innocent children. Mother and not even the devil himself would forgive them. They will not see the pests we got rid of. There's a neigh chance they would have grown to accept people like me and Misty. Don't we deserve to live the way we want to live? If we show our true self they would be more than willing to hurl us out of existence. How is it that only we have to be moral, non-judgemental and sympathetic while they always move in the opposite direction? I guarantee that the severity of punishment for the same crime committed by us and them would be different. Who is the one being wronged? US!*

Reena saw a sudden change in her son's face. It went red all over stretching up to his ears. The veins on his temple popped out. His nostrils flared and the eyes widened. Something was playing in his mind and it wasn't good.

"Hey calm now. What's bothering you?" Reena spoke softly and with a bit of fear. *He really scares me. I wouldn't want to be on the receiving end of his wrath. Oh! God! The senior he beat up. If he could do that then what else he is capable of now shudder's me.*

Aavi held his tongue. He didn't trust himself. He was fuming from within. Any action of his would only be vile in nature. He walked up to the water pot, poured himself a glass of water and drank it. It was a cold night and so was the water and it froze him from within as he had gulped it down. For the time being he stood there before stretching his muscular body to crack some bones. The crackling was too loud in this dark hour and sent a chill down Reena's spine. *He really frightens me.*

"We need someone else to take the fall. I can't think of any other alternative for you to escape." Reena broke the eerie silence.

"Do you have anyone in mind?"

"No. I don't know anyone else who had beef with Lath. As far as this village is concerned, he was an upstanding citizen, that bastard. "

"I agree, a bastard." Aavi chuckled.

"You know to this day I am in disbelief that he took advantage of our situation. I went into his office hoping we could have a talk. I knew you were in big trouble. I feared the cops being involved and even if they weren't he couldn't just let you walk out without a severe punishment. Deep down I guess most men only want one thing, Women to fuck without consequences."

"MOM..!"

"We are past being shy about things. And it's more of a fact."

"I'm sorry you had to go through that because of me. I really enjoyed tearing him apart."

What!!!!!!

For a jiffy Aavi went back to that gratifying night. Rage drove him to those events. A mistake the way he picked Lath right in front of a few passers-by, the only fault that day. Rest of it was deeply soothing, satisfying and amusing.

There is something seriously wrong with my boy. Tore him apart!! What the heck does it even mean? Did he literally rip Lath up? He could do that. He has unbelievable strength. Oh God! Help my son. Look at him. Look at that victorious face. He doesn't regret it one bit. I need to save him from this dire situation and then from himself. He needs to learn forgiveness and forgive himself.

"We need someone who is far from innocent. Sending an honest person to jail would weigh us down. A guy who at one point or other had a brawl with Lath or anyone with a history of violence would do the job." There were too many ideas swimming in her head and Reena tried catching up with them. It was a shamble up there, a desperate measure to save her son.

"Don't stress out. I will find a solution. There's always one. "

"There may be but would it be in time to save you?" Reena was freaking out. It was hard enough that her image in this village was trash. Once these accusations are known they will not be shunned, they will be either hunted or left somewhere to die, no, rot.

"I better come up with something real fast."

You better.

CHAPTER TWENTY-FOUR

Dinaat was back to a place he swore off not to ever step foot unless on official business. It was three in the morning! Sleep eluded him. His focus was lost to the needs of the flesh. Flashes of Reena's slightly exposed chest up to her neck tormented his body. He had noticed he made her uncomfortable and tried to sway his gaze. Reena was beautiful and easy to be attracted to. It was evident earlier in the day and an hour ago too as her image made it impossible for him to rest. So he walked away disregarding the cold weather to his happy place. Not anymore though. A little more than two years had passed when in this very place he broke his wife's heart. He had no case to argue.

Dinaat cheated on his wife over and over again albeit with only one person for nearly two months before being caught. He loved Sukanya from the very moment he saw her. Followed her like a stalker to her house where her husband broke off his building infatuation. It was more than being infatuated he realized. He needed to talk to her anyhow. So he pretended to walk to her house to question her about an on-going investigation while her husband was out for work or whatever.

A rock fell and broke him on knowing what she actually did. Understandably it was all her husband's doing. But one look at her and all his love renewed. She looked and was innocent as a dove, perfect description for her. Fair and gentle from the outside and paddling away from within to keep herself sane from all the atrocities she suffered on a daily basis. *No more* Dinaat pledged. He would protect her. Fly her away. He would leave his wife and kid.

Married to a stranger at that adolescent age when the most important thing to him was to bunk classes and hang out was simply wrong. Over the years he enjoyed his wife's company. He took good care of her. Even she couldn't say otherwise and if they were true to themselves, they never had any kind of spark between them. Their relationship was based on formalities. A pretence to the public eyes of the love they shared contrary to how they never missed each other's company.

Sukanya, as Dinaat expected, didn't share his endearment. She was pleased that he was gentle and consumed hours after hours of her time. At first she believed he would free her. How naive of her to fathom that? Dinaat could see her disappointment. He was dejected. Courage was what he couldn't muster to break her free when he found out about her prime customer, Shaanu.

Once he solves this case Dinaat pledged to go all out against Shaanu. He has been a nuisance for far too long and Dinaat was responsible for it too. Over the years their paths intertwined and Dinaat had to bend against his will. It was and is still embarrassing that the police force gave a thug the opportunity to overpower them. Sworn to protect the country and do the right thing. What a lie! It was time to live by those words.

No one answered the loud thumping of the wooden door. It was strange. Sukanya's husband (he couldn't remember his name) always responded. That greedy drunk would rush on a broken limb to welcome potential customers. After Shaanu is dealt with he was putting him behind bars.

Dinaat became aware of the hushed surrounding and ceased his knocking lest a neighbour or two woke up. He went around the house to try his luck. A sneak peek from an open window could possibly clear this little mystery. Everything was shut, even stranger. He came back to the front and restrained himself from kicking off the door. That's when he saw the rusty old lock on the handle. *Nope something's definitely wrong. That leech isn't going to take a vacation.*

Did he sell her to some bloke and took off? Unfortunately it had to be considered. No one knows what a person is truly capable of. He seated himself on one of the two narrow steps leading to Sukanya's door. It was ice cold and he shivered. He was in his dirty bluish green pyjamas and a knitted red yellow sweater which failed to cover his bulging belly. This protruding fat a few years ago would have given him sleepless nights. Now all he could think was *to hell with it*. His lack of interest and concern for everything made him invisible. When his wife left and took their daughter with her, guiltiness overpowered him. They were not coming back and he couldn't free Sukanya. Dinaat became miserable, nothing pleased him and nothing made him happy or even smile. People with their regular life seemed to have a luxury he would never have and being around them was out of compulsion of the job and not out of willingness.

Dinaat was bugged by the absence of any onlookers. Here they were a group of policemen forcing entry in a house in a crowded neighbourhood and not a single person around the area was curious enough to know what was happening.

What was wrong with these people? Where was the compassion for Sukanya? No one can tell that she willingly threw herself in the arms of strangers. She screamed and begged for those monsters to stop. He had heard it in the first month of his visit. He couldn't be with her all the time so Dinaat extended his stay as long as he could. He delayed the cruelness done to her. He should have stopped it. His head hung in shame and regret as he searched her cage. Normally with the bed sheet all wrinkled and not well tucked one could assume that maybe there was a struggle. Here, it could never be considered. Sukanya's bed was always roughed up. Apart from that everything else was how it should be. Nothing else was out of order and none of the things seemed to be missing. After breaking into the wardrobe it was confirmed that they had not run away. All their clothes and money were well kept. Dinaat feared the worst, Murder.

CHAPTER TWENTY-FIVE

Last night was fun, wild and insane. Misty promised he would make it up to Onik after Misty accidentally revealed that he and Aavi were having fun of their own. Onik was aware of their adventure; he had no desire of being a part of it. It was all a part of Misty's grand scheme to put Aavi on a leash. What a waste of time. Onik was going to undo everything that Misty was striving for. He had spent too much time in and around this circus. Onik didn't mean to join Misty and Aavi in their killing business. He improvised to save himself. Somehow he was into it. No sense of guilt took over. It made it easier for him to blend in. He lost track of his aim. It was time to start the beginning of the end.

It was almost seven when Onik and Misty met at the abandoned bridge. From there Onik rode with Misty in Misty's car to the nearest town.

"Where to now..?" Misty asked.

"Let's find a bar."

"I don't drink."

"Does it look like I do? I want to check what the fuss is about."

"It will be a waste of time. Foul smell accompanied by foul breath and if we are lucky we witness a drunken fool blabbering or getting involved in a fight."

"You seem to know a lot for a person who doesn't drink?"

"I said I don't drink. I didn't say I haven't been to these places, have I?"

They asked around and a local directed them to a shop that sold liquor. Ostensibly there were no bars in this town. Few more minutes of driving placed them almost at the edge of the town. Misty and Onik squinted to search for the shop. Left, right, straight and sometimes backwards they looked. They half expected to see a line somewhere. A cue to where the shop was. The shutters were down for most of the shops and a few were closing for the day. The car moved at a tortoise pace for about ten minutes before Onik spotted the seller who was going to kick start their outing.

Misty sat back at the driver's seat and took out the Jack Daniels from the brown paper bag. Onik snatched the brownish liquid glass bottle and eyed it. He opened it quickly and took a sip. As the liquid touched his tongue Onik quickly rolled down the window to his right and spat it out.

"It's awful." Onik spat some more trying to cleanse his tongue from Jack Daniels.

Misty had no intention of tasting it from the onset. Onik's reaction glued his lips even further.

"That bad, huh, " said Misty.

"I need to get rid of this taste."

"Now what...?" Misty asked, ignoring Onik's discomfort.

"Drive on. I will tell you to stop if I see something," said Onik, quite vexed.

Misty drove around aimlessly and slowly. He felt Onik was exaggerating his reaction to the liquor. Every now and then he spat out of the window and made disgusting faces.

"Stop..." Onik said out aloud.

The tires hadn't screeched to halt before Onik somewhat rolled out on the street. Onik jerked his jacket off of dirt and pulled himself up. Then he headed towards a vagrant who lay on the side of the road. It was dead silent all around. No people and no dogs. Not a single source of light from the surrounding shops and houses except from a distant street light. Its pole bent down and it's light flickering.

"Hey, get up." Onik shook the vagrant's shoulder to wake him up. "You can't be sleeping out here in the cold. Do you want to freeze to death? Come with me I will take you to a place with a roof and walls. It's your lucky night."

The vagrant got up bewildered and followed Onik to Misty's car.

"I'm not letting this dirty old scum in my car. He could be carrying diseases we haven't even heard of." Misty protested.

"I promised him shelter. Now be a good citizen and help a fellow out."

"You are out of your fucking mind. I'm not letting him in."

"Can you see what people think of you?"

The vagrant who was half asleep didn't care, he was promised shelter and he was waiting for it.

When he got no response Onik pushed the vagrant down the road. The vagrant stumbled and hit the paved road hard and squealed.

"I asked you a question. Answer you dimwit." Onik continued his assault, stomping on the vagrant and rubbing the sole of his shoes on the vagrant's face.

"You idiot, someone will wake up." Misty hushed in anger.

"Stop being such a control freak. Learn to do what you want without caring for people." Onik responded.

"I'm not kidding, kid. Get in now before someone wakes up."

"Promise me we are killing someone."

"Obviously you are an idiot. Why do you think I'm spending this night with you?"

Ten minutes of driving led Misty and Onik to the slum part of the town. In the summer it was easy for Misty to pick up his next victim. These people usually slept with their door open to let any sort of air in or on the outside to avoid the hot chamber their home became. Misty didn't have the guts to take any kid sleeping next to their parents or siblings. He waited for any of them to take a leak or whatever. Anything that made sure that they were not in the vicinity of anyone. Usually he got lucky by picking strays on the side of the road. Sometimes he didn't and the urge was too strong to get rid off. It stuck to him like superglue. He couldn't rinse it off without doing anything. He had to take a life. Winter was different and difficult. No one wandered around late at night and everyone slept with their doors shut. He had to capture them during the fading daylight, bind them in the trunk of his car whilst he enjoyed family time. Wait for his wife to be sound asleep and then sneak off. She wouldn't budge with his desire to drive around during the weather that would bind him sick to bed.

Onik stepped out of the vehicle and took in the foul smell of garbage and piss. It was simply sad and awful that people had to live in such places. Irrespective of what money people have, everyone deserved to live in a clean and fresh environment. Onik could see himself as an angel freeing these kids from the stench, a permanent solution to the never ending misery of being poor. No thoughts, no pain and no worries.

The silver light shone across the tin of the crowded slum houses. The houses were lined up in five rows and didn't extend much further to the back. Onik wasn't going to wait around for some kid to wander around. It also seemed like a very foolish thing for even a kid to do. Onik went around checking which of the doors was unlocked. Misty was anxious but didn't protest. There was a curiosity in him to see how this would pan out. The revolver tucked behind Onik's back gave him the confidence of escape after being caught. He was ready to test their luck.

Onik was nearly done with all of the doors. It was irking him and exasperation crawled all along his skin. This night wasn't supposed to be a black and white one. He came here to fill his world with red. He took a deep breath and prayed that this crooked door was unlocked. There was a creak. His heart jumped. Steadily, slowly and carefully Onik drew the door across the one room house. The room wasn't filled with light as the moon was on the other side. A family of four slept straight ahead on the mud floor, the husband and wife in each other's arms and their two boys to the left of the mother. One seemed two years of age and the other five. Both slept in an identical fashion, curling their body and legs up. They both looked like a question mark.

Steadily Onik placed his right arm under the five year old neck. Quickly he covered the young mouth and in a quick motion grabbed the kid with his left. The kid awakened and squirmed. Onik held him tight and subdued his voice and movements. Misty followed Onik's head movement, gesturing for him to pick the tiny one. Misty did it on a whim or else he was sure to mess everything up. He became jealous of Onik's authority and courage. It wasn't the time to dwell on it and he focused on the kid at hand.

Once they stepped out they quickened their movement and when they reached the old dusty car they got a sense of relief.

"Give me the kid and quickly start the engine."

Onik held the tiny one with his left. A little yelp was all the kid could manage while Onik adjusted his left palm across the kid's mouth. No damage done. Misty opened the back door for Onik and closed it once Onik was in. He then quickly got in the driver's seat and drove off.

The kids went wild as soon as Onik released his grasp. Yelling on top of their voices and kicking and punching with their full strength. It took a minute for Onik to reinforce control. He slapped the kids savagely leaving traces of his fingers on their soft thin skins.

"Hand me the Jack Daniels."

"Are you sure?"

"It's for them."

Misty was left stunned. It was outright devilish. He wondered for a moment how different his life would have been if Onik was his age and they had grown up together, lively and short.

Onik forced the liquid down the elder's throat. Once Onik shoved the neck of the bottle in the opening of the kid's mouth there was no struggle. Continuous stream of tears flowed down the cheeks to the leather seat. Onik held the heavy glass bottle till its content drained out. Misty had ceased driving to watch the spectacle.

"We have a drinking master." Onik declared.

"You are going to hell for that."

"Living is hell."

"True. Now what? "

"Drive as fast as you can."

Misty wasn't going to burn the wheels. It was scary to see a car breeze past. He focused on his lane. He never overtook a vehicle in front of him. His wife didn't approve of his over the top carefulness. Many times he got honked at by the vehicles behind him and when they overtook they bad mouthed him. Misty didn't partake in those altercations. He held his tongue lest he wanted to shame himself in front of a crowd.

The speedometer clocked sixty and by far this was his best. Misty held the speed along the smooth road.

"What's your plan?"

"Now I throw the kid out of this speeding car, ready for some action?"

"Hey wait. Throw him from the left door. I want to watch."

"You sure..? If I do that you will only watch me throw him out. Not anything afterwards. I throw him from the right so you get to see everything in the side mirror."

"Right..." *Dumb.*

Onik opened the gate and held it while pushing the kid out. The young one was pulling his shirt from the back as if that tiny force he could accumulate was of any use. The elder didn't protest. He was drunk and lost somewhere, not aware of what was happening to him. The first attempt went horribly wrong. Onik couldn't muster the strength with his right arm to throw the kid out in one go. Jack Daniels had added weight to the kid. Only the kid's head popped outside the moving car. Onik lost control of the door and it swung in strong and fast.

Snap.

Onik did limit the damage done. He tried pulling the kid back up. Instead of hitting the top of the skull the door slammed on the back.

"Where is he? I can't see him," said Misty alarmingly, unaware of the incident.

"Relax. The kid's still here. It's not like he's going to run away. And even if he did it won't affect us. I lost control of the door; it swung back before I could throw him out. Keep your eye on the side mirror if you don't want to miss the show." Onik was miffed. The younger one continued his futile attempt to stop Onik. For a while Onik had forgotten about him. He was lost in his actions. He slapped the young one, hard, two three times and the sobbing came loud and shrill.

Misty was focused on the road ahead and checked the side mirror simultaneously. The gate opened once more. He looked ahead and then back at the side mirror. The door was closed and he saw the kid roll backwards, spinning far out from his view. It was a brief period yet it was something entirely different and added to the thrill of the night.

"Let's check him out."

Misty was curious to see the damage done.

"Nah, keep driving. He won't go anywhere. You can stare at his body when you return. We have more to do."

CHAPTER TWENTY-SIX

Aavi was restless. Before the start of the summer to now, in between winter, he was two different people. However he tried to justify his actions over this period with Misty it all came down to one conclusion - He, Aavi, was a child killer. It shook him a little. From being a witness to a participant had disturbingly taken only a few days. How good did it feel though? His lips curled upward on remembering his first kill night. It even broke his curse of sleepless nights. And since the past few days it was back.

The conversation with his Mom developed a bit of guilty conscience. He lied, lied and lied thoroughly to his Mom when they were supposedly being honest. It was nagging him at the back of his head. It was evident she knew he was spinning her around in his false tales. She didn't question him lest she angers him, Aavi assumed. A mother shouldn't fear her son or vice versa. He could see how affectionate she tried to be with him all these years and how distant he was. How could he bore so much disgust for her when she was the one cleaning up his mess? Whatever hell life threw at him he never found a way to tackle it the right way. He needed to blame someone and what better person than your loved ones?

His mother *knew* him. All these years he thought he was alone, he couldn't share. The answer was right in his home. How could he be so stupid to not trust his Mom?

If only. The stars would take him to a different path, a path without Misty. Would he have a place for someone other than Misty? NO. Good or bad, right or wrong nothing mattered. No one could ignite in him what Misty did. He chose Misty. He belonged with him.

Once more Aavi was at his favourite spot. The vast expanse of greenery even in this cruel weather spoke thunderously that he belonged here. Away from civilization was his place. Ah! He missed those lonely days, staring into the night sky searching for answers or drowning in his sorrows and sometimes basking in pleasant thoughts. There was peace in it and to have someplace with no interference is worth a lot. One needs to be alone for a certain time in a day to reflect or simply be devoid of anything. Aavi missed it more than he realized.

One night and everything changed. His sanctuary tainted, disrupted and surrendered willingly for human companionship. Was this a betrayal or was it understandable that Aavi needed to prioritize his basic needs? He was happy. He was allowed to, wasn't he?

Aavi dawdled towards the abandoned bridge, brooding. His head ducked, shoulders lifted and enclosed towards the body and his hands inside the pitch black jacket's pocket. His apparel wasn't thick and didn't provide enough warmth for this freezing weather. The gravel road was unfit to walk for the preoccupied, especially in this dark. It was no longer a smooth layer or an even surface. What remained were potholes of various sizes and depths. Naturally Aavi walked on the side of the road. The grass was wet and his leisurely walk ensured his foot didn't slip. A few metres away on either side of the road large teak trees ran along in great numbers. Numerous birds resided on them.

A wave of cold shock ran through Aavi as he lay on the edge of the broken bridge. It took his body a while to cease shuddering. His mind kept calling him an 'Idiot' for leaving the warmth of four walls and a roof. It was better than dwelling on the subject of morality and the consequences of his decisions. Even though his vile choices brought peaceful sleep over the summer, Aavi didn't feel rested. Something was missing and he couldn't ascertain as to what it was.

What a soft mattress, a cozy blanket and a warm environment couldn't do a hard rough surface out in the open did it with ease. Aavi slept.

The sound of a car engine woke Aavi up. He was cold all over and felt his temperature soar. His immediate thought was to return back and glue himself to wool. It was almost dawn and the sky was grey and the birds flew across in numbers. The engine was brought to a halt and Aavi wasn't startled. It had to be Misty. Aavi was slightly surprised. Typically Misty texted or called him before coming here. Misty never did come by himself after their first meeting except that one time for Onik. He hastily took out his cell and checked for any missed calls or text. There were none. Aavi heard two different sounds of laughter. This actually made him sicker, Onik. There was something unexplainable about Onik that made Aavi's skin crawl. His face always plainly stated his emotions. He never hid it nor did consider putting on a friendly face. Nothing good could come from Onik's companionship.

Aavi got up and headed towards the other side of the broken bridge. The ground was wet and slippery and he walked cautiously. His limbs and body were tensed and it added to his discomfort and the slowness of his walk. He could hear peals of laughter. Aavi was apprehensive of what lay ahead. Something wicked and evil was about to take place beyond the murder of a child.

It took Aavi ages to get up to the other half of the broken bridge. On the way up there, in his wobbly state, Aavi managed to get a few minor cuts and dirt all over his palm and face. His body gave up and he lay flat on the moist grass, panting, like he had run a mile. He stiffened his body and legs and his bones cracked and gave him momentary relief. The sky had turned bright grey and the surroundings could be seen clearly.

Misty and Onik were on about something. Aavi couldn't hear properly. They obviously didn't notice him or they would have passed on a sly remark. Aavi pulled up his body with what remaining strength he possessed. He never felt so weak. He was covered in sweat and he didn't like one bit how his clothes stuck to his skin. Aavi thought of calling Misty out. Instead he just walked straight towards them.

"Look, who we have here!" exclaimed Onik.

Misty turned around. His face immediately covered in guilt. It went without saying. Aavi's abhorrence towards Onik was well known to Misty. This was a betrayal.

Aavi never wondered how alike Misty and Onik were appearance wise. Right now all he could see was how they matched perfectly like brothers. Both had an average height with a lean and non-muscular body. Their long face with little facial hair, pointed nose, sharp ears and thin pinkish lips could easily pass them as brothers and not a single question would be raised. Their reasoning was similar too making them of one mind with two separate bodies.

"What are you two up to?" Aavi sounded weak.

"A little bit of mischief and fun." Onik grinned and looked like an undersized devil.

"You don't look well. Go home. Have you been here all night?"

"Aww, the concern..." Onik teased.

"What is that?"

"Toys...!"

Aavi went ahead and pushed Onik aside. What he saw turned his head upside down. Murdering a kid was still somewhat fine. It wasn't a cruel fate. Severing a child limb by limb couldn't justify anything. It was simply inhumane.

"Have you two completely lost it?" Aavi yelled. "I bet it was his idea." Aavi forced a punch at Onik and missed. Onik expected what was coming and simply ducked before time.

"Go home Aavi. This doesn't concern you. We are not bound to you. We can do what we want, when we want and how we want. Your permission or your presence isn't required. If you want to be with us then you need to swallow up your pride pill and help us."

All Aavi heard was WE, WE, WE and each WE had his heart in tethers. Onik was not even remotely close to their colour. He could never be in the 'WE'. He was in the 'WE'. He had to be in the 'WE'. Without WE what was HE?

Nothing...

"AAVI"

"What?"

"Go home."

"No."

"Don't act childish. It's freezing and you look pale and weak."

"Still can take you two and knock your asses out."

In no time Onik moved, swiftly, a sudden blistering pace, the revolver in his hand with the butt of it facing Aavi.

One two three and so on he struck Aavi, right on his face.

"You speak a lot Aavi. I have been patient long enough. You really think we need you. You fucking prick."

The first blow had nearly knocked Aavi out. He fell, head first and before he could cry out in pain Onik beat him. He then lost consciousness.

"Leave him. He's senseless."

"Not that easily. For far too long he has humiliated us. We may not have his physical robustness but I swear to you we don't need this bastard. We got this." Onik gestured at his revolver. "I know you want him in some other ways. You will find someone else. There are plenty in hiding. You can scout them with your senses."

That's not how it works, you idiot.

"I want you to beat him." Onik saw the hesitation in Misty and said, "Not like he's waking up." Onik punched Aavi to prove his point. "Do it." He emphasised.

Misty was obsessed with Aavi. Whether there was love or not he couldn't be entirely sure. He desired Aavi, undeniably. Did he care for him? There was a question mark. Past or present Misty plunged instantly in making decisions that would hurt Aavi. Even now he itched to do some damage to the immobile Aavi. Only the possibility of Aavi waking up held him back.

"Do it." Onik repeated. "If he gets up I will charge him with my revolver."

First Misty laid a weak punch. His heart began to palpitate and his hands trembled and his lips quivered. Sweat droplets appeared on his forehead. What was this, Fear or Love? Misty couldn't comprehend. Misty glanced at Onik who expressed his urge for Misty to man up.

It was time for Misty to break free and create havoc, to let go of the dread of being overpowered and be willing to face pain.

CHAPTER TWENTY-SEVEN

Onik was tempted to break Misty's nap. They had been awake all night. It was wise that he didn't. Misty had finally been pushed off the ledge and there was no way he and Aavi were ever going to be a team. It wasn't difficult separating these two clowns, quite easier than Onik anticipated.

"Wake up," shouted Onik at Misty's left ear. He had given Misty ample time to rest his old bones.

The loud voice did not startle Misty. He simply woke like he normally did and eyed Onik.

"Get up. We have work to do. It's judgement day." Onik still had a feeling of rush and adrenaline in him. He was excited for this day. At long last everything he planned for was going to unfold and he could have his peace. He would miss this journey but he would not lose his sleep over it.

Misty wasn't sure what judgement Onik was on about. Last night was fun, morning was a revelation and what was next would be a surprise.

The railing was freezing cold. Onik gripped it tightly and surrendered himself to the view of this abandoned place, greenery all around and a river flowing right through the mid of it, azure sky, no clouds and golden illumination all over. If a picture was taken it could be hung up on the walls of the living room. What lay underneath the soil was a horror story. What did it matter? What lies beneath a beauty has never been of importance. We live in a world of showiness.

Misty stood beside Onik and broke his trance. Onik then stretched his arms out and grabbed one of the torn arms of their victim. He backed a few paces, ran the small distance and threw the arm as far as he could with the momentum he gathered. Onik was satisfied with his effort. He was winning this game.

"You are a wicked person, you know that."

The two killers exchanged a smile and Misty played the game.

The rules were simple. There were six parts in total of the severed boy. Each would throw all six of them one after the other. The other person would be out there in the open and mark the greatest distance thrown of the parts. Once done he would collect and bring them back up and take his turn.

The game didn't last long. Misty grew tired after picking all the remains and carrying them up to the bridge on the very first time. Onik did throw one of the parts further than any of their total collective efforts. He rejoiced his win by yelling out some cuss words right on the face of the unmoving Aavi.

"Have you had your fun? Is there anything else?"

"Do you want to relax now old man?"

Misty gave him a no nonsense look.

"Chill out grandpa!"

"Keep that mouth of yours in check. One day someone's going to smash it."

"Not if I smash him first."

"A 'her' can smash it too."

"I will steal her heart."

"That's what will spark it."

"How do you know?"

"You being you I can't see any other outcome."

"Then I will push her off the cliff. Relieve it."

HAHAHAHAHA...

Onik spat on Aavi before leaving to carry out the one final activity he had in store for a long time.

"What are we doing here?" Misty was bewildered. This wasn't a good idea.

"What the numerous strangers in the past have done." Onik replied.

"You are out of your mind. We will not survive."

"Now why are you always so scared? Haven't we gotten away with things that people don't even think to do in their wildest dreams. And you, you have carried on with your dark deeds for years, living your life like a normal individual whilst not your colleagues or even your wife suspect you of any foul play."

"This is different. This will get us caught. This will be the end for both of us." Misty couldn't have warned him enough for his upcoming actions.

"I don't care. I want to do this and I will, even if it means the end of me. I would like you to join me."

"There's nothing to achieve here. Only thing it will accomplish is our destruction. And why would I walk knowingly to my end."

"We aren't walking to our end. The consequences of it will obviously be severe. Though I feel we are big enough to tackle it. And didn't we beat the shit out of him a few hours ago?"

"This is too risky, I'm not going in."

"What else can be expected of a coward like you?"

Onik was bleeding from the nose in no time.

"I told you, you speak way too much. You try extra hard to show that you take me for a coward. I know you don't. I can't figure out what is it that you have against Aavi. From the time we have met, you have tried to instigate and provoke me against him. You know very well how I feel about him. There's both hate and love. One outshines the other according to my mood. Right now I have hurt him thanks to you and yet I have no regrets. I fall into your trap willingly. Don't assume otherwise. You aren't clever enough. This though is going too far. I'm not going to get involved."

"Wait. Don't leave. Hear me out."

"Can we come in?"

"I'm not going to fuck you in my house. Find a place and call me. I will be there." Reena ran her mouth. She wasn't usually vocal. The kid in front of her was arrogant. The man beside him was silent. They looked like father and son or two brothers with years apart.

"I don't understand what the problem is. Everyone knows who you are. What the fuck do you care where you fuck?"

"There's nothing for you to understand. You want my service you need to follow my rules." She prayed for them to leave without creating a fuss. They looked weak yet they oozed danger, evil dancing in their eyes. She didn't want to be anywhere around them.

"Do you fear us?" asked the kid.

"No." She failed to say it convincingly. Her face had gone pale and there was an involuntary movement of her limbs.

"Oh I'm sorry if I come across rude or desperate. It's the way I am. People misunderstand me. My friend here can vouch for it."

"He is an arrogant little bastard." Misty relished saying these words.

"See." This little charade somewhat cooled Reena.

"Come on. Let us in," insisted Onik.

"No. Rules are rules."

Onik shoved Reena inside with one strong push. Misty closed the gate instantly. Reena crawled backwards with her hand fearing for her life.

"Don't be scared. We only want to know what's so special about you that men cheat on their wives."

Reena had lost her voice. All that mattered was for them to be miles away from her. She didn't want to encounter them even coincidentally.

"I guess she's a believer in action speaks louder than words."

Misty laughed uncontrollably.

CHAPTER TWENTY-EIGHT

FINALLY IT WAS OVER!! Physically, yes. Mentally, NEVER!! This was the kind of incident that propels one to take one's life. Reena couldn't even bother to move a muscle. She was in complete shock. Her breathing disgusted her. Everything was meant to be over. That's how it should have been after what happened. Life was a curse. It never could be or was heavenly, now it will be hell. How could answering a door close the doors to life? How fragile life is? How terrible things can happen on a whim? Why do we even call it life? It should be renamed as something that describes it as misery, depressing and how big a joke you are made to be.

Reena has been slapped around, only playfully and only in the bedroom. Sometimes she enjoyed it sometimes it was strictly for business, nothing extreme and always below her tolerance level. She didn't want to walk around with a mark on her skin. Few men enjoyed to exert their dominance on at least one lady in their life. Reena gave them that pleasure and happiness they derived from being in control. Today she didn't have her customers at her clutch. Meek and weak they looked. Overpowering and strong they emerged.

Once those hounds entered her home, her sanctuary, Reena didn't feel safe. She cried for help, none came. She threw inanimate objects, she missed. Everything and everyone seemed to be against her, the former a no brainer and neither surprising. Betrayed by her willingness to fight shook her. Those scoundrels kept punching and slapping her wherever they could lay their hands on. Yet no surge of energy overflew from her to keep any sort of these attacks at bay. Any attempt to play dead failed terribly as they continued their heinous act in a way that would imprint everything in her brain. The very room that brought her solace would only be a measure of sorrow.

When any unfortunate event befalls us we immediately raise our head and question God, Why? We may have led our life to that point like a saint or a devil and the question still remains as to why it's happening to me? Saint or devil doesn't matter, every individual makes mistakes. Some way or the other our actions or words inflicts pain to someone, minor or major makes no difference. When we face these unfortunate challenges we realize or blame ourselves for what we may have done. This is payback, all the way from above while we are living. We are punished while we can feel, in this life itself and not beyond. Reena for the better part of her life had subjected families to quarrel. It was obvious even though there wasn't any proof. Her attackers put a bit of truth to it. 'What's so special about you that men cheat on their wives?'

A crime was being committed. Generally there's a motive behind every vile act by people. Reena had aggrieved the younger sinner, she knew not how. He was very vocal, spewing venom out of his mouth even before he began to physically assault her. Reena had faced quite a number of men in her life, tall, short, lanky, stout, shy, aggressive, shrewd, stupid, and funny and many more. Today perhaps for the first time she met someone she considered dangerous right from the word go. Of all the things, situation and men she should have been afraid of, a teenager was out of the blue. The moment she laid her eyes on him his whole aura screamed, 'I'm bad news.'

At first Reena was confused as to why he was doing what he was doing to her. She avoided looking at him. It wasn't for long. She met his eyes with her swollen one and stared. He cussed her for gazing and hit her hard on her already distorted face. Obstinately she continued to gawk inviting unnecessary harm to herself. Reena did cast doubt in her attacker's mind. He hesitated, ceased momentarily, shook his head and resumed. It was like he had to do it even if it was disturbing and wrong. This struck Reena. She concentrated more on her tormentor's countenance. The realization that dawned on her caused turmoil in her head. 'What's so special about you that men cheat on their wives?" Everything was now crystal clear.

Actions have consequences. Reena's came in a cruel form. She deserved some punishment. Not this. No one ever deserves this. This was devastating and earth shattering and beyond repair, a permanent damage to her mind and soul. There's a saying, 'It all happened so fast.' For Reena it was an eternity, never ending, physical pain alongside a humongous mental one. There was nothing left for her now. She wanted to remain at the corner of her room where she sat with her arms around her knees to her chest, never to move from there and never to sleep. If someone could turn her into a stone it would be the greatest mercy one could lay upon her. God wasn't going to do that. God had already let the hurricane ravage her and if that wasn't enough they left her with information that left no measure for her to ever recover.

Reena comprehended that the barbaric teenager was trying to teach her a lesson for uprooting his parent's life. The other person had made himself invisible to the extent that Reena forgot that he was there too. When she became aware of his presence she saw he was only acting as a spectator. He seemed to only tag along, to join the fun, to witness his compatriot's wickedness. It was all too transparent for Reena how enjoyable the whole circumstance was for him and it made her jittery. Her intuition kicked in. Nope. He wasn't an onlooker. He was savouring this moment, filling his heart and mind with images of her destruction but for what? To brag, to hurt and to whom, her SON!

"This isn't even the worst thing happening to you." The man said after the teenager had finished his business. "Have you heard about the missing principal, a daughter and a father? Well they are all dead. And there are even more to that list, all children, KIDS and a few teenagers, murdered! Your son Aavi did it. I made him do it. He's an idiot by the way. All muscles no brain, followed me like I'm his Daddy. You should have married someone so that he could look up to him growing up. Maybe he wouldn't have been so desperate to gain someone's approval. You really fucked up." He gloated and his eyes danced in excitement as he uttered those words. Then they left and Reena was torn and lost.

CHAPTER TWENTY-NINE

Aavi had to put quite an effort to lift himself up after the beating he endured. The state of his body wasn't good either. He was burning in the midst of cold breeze and grey sky. His cheeks were all puffed up and it burned whenever the wind blew past him. The swollen cheeks obstructed his vision and for once he thought that Onik had done some permanent damage to his eyes. His head was heavy and it constantly weighed him down to the ground. He had to hold his head for a while to keep it steady. There was a deep gash on his forehead that ran down to his nose but the blood had ceased to ooze out. A similar cut was on the back of his head and it hurt terribly.

Aavi didn't remember much of it and neither did he try to recall. He didn't need to. Onik and Misty beat the living shit out of him. That was it. All that actually mattered was WHY? From the onset of meeting Onik their hostility for one another was no secret. Onik always looked for trouble with him. Baiting and teasing him for reasons unknown. He clearly wanted to cause a rift between him and Misty since he interfered in their life. Yes that's what it was, an intrusion and a planned one. Else how can one explain the extraordinary coincidence of Onik killing a person while they were doing it too? Why would Onik even do that when he knew Aavi would have questions about the missing girl? It was fishy then and so were his intentions even now. Onik had successfully infiltrated and separated him and Misty.

Misty: the idiot.

Misty for whom he turned a blind eye upon everything...

Misty for whom he left morality...

Misty for whom he became a killer...

He gave up so much to satisfy his need for love and to be loved. People really do lose their ability to distinguish right from wrong when they want something or someone. How can one all of a sudden be impassive to everyone or everything else? How can one forget to question themselves? If one doesn't reflect on their actions, what's stopping them from crossing a line? And Aavi did much more than that. He uprooted everything. Where the hell was his common sense? How could he have failed himself so effortlessly? Who was the actual fool?

Aavi was ill, weak and hurting, broken from outside and inside. He was physically hurt but mentally awoken. Both Onik and Misty were sick, twisted, cruel and evil. Both lured him in, in their own devious way and Aavi fell right into it.

To descend the abandoned bridge and ascend to the other part felt like a life threatening walk. Aavi had his heart out. He took a deep breath and the smell of dried blood welcomed him, which ran from his nose to his lip and to his chin. One step he took and the other and every other step so on came with a sharp pain. Aavi's body crumbled against his weight. Like some aged person he trudged with a crouched back. He picked up a long and strong enough stick on his way and his transformation to old age was complete.

The short familiar path had turned long and weary. Aavi was exhausted. He stumbled, cried out in pain and cursed everything and everyone in exasperation. The sight of *Otto* was a big relief after what seemed like an eternity of walking. Hurriedly he seated himself at the back seat, rested his back against the comfy leather and dozed off.

Coldness spread all over Aavi as he parked *Otto* in the small makeshift garage. There were no street lights in this part of the village and though it was only nearly an hour past sunset one would think it was time for the wolves to howl. Nothing but dread filled Aavi as he walked up the steps to his house. The lights were out and the door was unlocked. Aavi's throat tightened and he forgot about his own painful sores.

"Mom," Aavi called out in a child-like voice. No answer. He stepped in and called her out again. No answer. Aavi didn't switch on the living room light. He was scared. He was sure he would see something that will scar him for life. His eyes had adjusted to the blackness and he could see that the door to her room was open. She wasn't in his visibility. He stepped in and went past the untidy bed. He was half expecting to find a pool of blood, his Mom lying dead on the floor with her neck sliced up. Yet the feeling of apprehension didn't leave him. He heard a whimper and to his left on the other side of the bed against the wall sat his Mom.

A ghost! That was what she looked like, a dead person in a living body. If he were a child right now he would have screamed in terror and never ever get up in the middle of the night. Though it was still evening, dread had seized his heart. She was very statue like. Head down with half of her hair covering her face which had lost its colour and shape. Her arms tightly wrapped around her knees, everything about her shrieked brutality.

What Aavi had gone through few hours ago was miniscule. It was only a bruise. He was already over it. This though was; mammoth. The person becomes extinct and their loved ones are helpless. Aavi suppressed the urge to hug his Mom. He couldn't speak or move a muscle and neither could he think straight. It was never ever safe for her. The world was filled with vile men. Aavi was one too. With Shaanu being with her, Aavi in a way was relieved that no harm would come to her at least from other sources. Not even a dangerous person can protect someone or something.

Words wouldn't leave Aavi's mouth. *Who did this? Who did this? WHO DID THIS?* The question kept circling in him. As much as he was brimming in anger he was distressed. When the person you love gets hurt that's when your true feelings surfaces. All the fights he'd had with his Mom could never wipe out the love he had for her. Nothing was more important to Aavi than her health and state of mind. All he could contribute as of now was to just be there. He sat down near her, patiently waiting for any sort of communication with his Mom.

"You did kill those kids, didn't you?" Reena's voice was low and shaky. In their last conversation the truth of it didn't escape her. Every parent would be hesitant to believe that their offspring is a killer. It's hard to accept the truth. One day there isn't an option left.

"I did. I was so angry at everyone and so full in love. Misty took undue advantage of me and I gave in. Love is blind and I'm a blind fool." There was honesty in his voice.

The house was on a silent notice once more. The tiny confession was enough for Reena and it was easy to figure out who this Misty was, the person who ruined her world. Aavi wasn't expecting it to be the first conversation of this awful day. A simple sentence like hold me, take my hand or an outcry of what was done.

"Mom, drink some water." Aavi decided to do something rather than sit idly and let sorrow overcome them. They needed any kind of distraction especially his mom. She had been put into a corner by some wild animal and Aavi had to free her.

Mom, this three letter word along with that child-like voice brought tears to Reena's eyes. *How sweet did he sound, my Aavi.* He said it exactly like this an hour or so ago and now again. If only he could say it in a loop. The horror of this day weighed like a gigantic mountain and to push it off her that innocent child-like voice of her son felt like a start. He had placed the glass of water near her feet. She wasn't thirsty. She drank it to not disappoint his effort.

"I will make us dinner."

I'm not hungry.

"I know you don't want to eat or do anything. Yet you must. You have to start somewhere."

I drank the water.

Aavi left the room and he switched on the living room lights. "We can't let darkness be our companion."

There were unclean utensils in the sink, last night's and this morning. Lunch wasn't prepared nor was there any preparations done for it. The unspoken incident took place after breakfast and at least an hour before their usual lunch timing. This discovery had no significance. Aavi had a fair idea as to who the perpetrator(s) were. He dismissed it as of now to focus on the task at hand.

Once the dishes were cleaned thoroughly Aavi began to make dinner. He had cooked before, nothing that would make anyone demand more out of taste. Mostly his meal would taste of salt and chilli. He prepared rice, daal and potato curry. The daal was in a much higher proportion to the other two. He overflew the daal in his mom's plate and before serving her he switched on the lights to her room. She immediately covered her deformed face with her hand to block the sudden brightness.

"The food is ready. You should eat." Aavi spoke and left to bring her plate.

Reena stared at her dinner. The rice and potato were drowning in a sea of daal. It was clever of her son to serve it like a soup. Her throat was extremely dry and she wouldn't be able to gulp down anything solid. It was a smart thing to do only if he could somehow bring back her appetite and her willingness to live. She didn't even want to move an inch of her body, forget picking up a plate of food and guzzling it down.

"Mom..."

Reena was startled. She was lost somewhere thinking about nothing. Her son's newly found childish voice broke her reverie. *Why couldn't he always say it like this?* It soothed her heart and gave it a breathing space. He was holding a spoonful of the food near her mouth urging her to eat. Involuntarily she let her son feed her. She glanced at him once or twice. He had a slight smile. Halfway through the course she had enough of it and refused by shaking her hands. Aavi didn't ask twice. He quietly got back to his plate and finished his dinner.

Aavi had scooched beside his Mom after dinner. He held her by his right arm and let her rest on his right shoulder. They required one another's presence especially Reena, and Aavi was there for her. She finally fell asleep while Aavi's nocturnal instinct kicked in. When he was certain she was asleep Aavi slowly picked her up and laid her on the bed. He covered her with the blanket and moved out of the room.

"How's your mom?" The text message from Onik sent over an hour ago read.

Onik, Onik, Onik. I'm gonna kill him. I'm gonna kill them both. Those bastards!

CHAPTER THIRTY

A pack of ferocious dogs of brown, black and white strode the lonely street as was their usual custom when the two legged was shut in. They snarled, chased one another and barked from time to time. It was their time and they did what pleased them. Mostly they searched for food in the garbage strewn all over the place where they usually resided. When they smelled something fishy they woofed out loud and ran after the smell. The upright beings were mostly kind. Few served them food and few petted them while passing by or when they lingered around the clothed beings.

My dad's been fucking your mom. You know where to find me.

Atrocious mouth and vile texting, Onik sure knew how to stir Aavi up. *That skinny bastard wants me to end him. I will gladly grant him his wish.*

Aavi was in disbelief on how he could have forgotten who Onik was, Shaanu's son. He was searching for WHY when everything was so obvious. The kid plotted everything and Aavi played a fools role to grant Onik his wish. How could he have not kept a close watch on Onik? How could he have not taken Onik seriously?

Paying no heed to what lay in front of him Aavi drove fast and recklessly. He was eager to get his hands on Onik. If it wasn't for Misty, Aavi would have bashed Onik long ago. Onik wouldn't have been a state to move a muscle and none of this would have occurred. Right now Aavi's eye shone with revenge and he was in a hurry to let everything out. His rash driving nearly hit one of the dogs that hung around the turning that led to Onik's home. The dog shrieked with terror, the others growled then barked, grew wild and chased after his *Otto*. Aavi hadn't witnessed such a wild pack of dogs. They didn't give up whether Aavi took a right or a left or drove further away than their territory. It was an exhilarating pursuit. Aavi was now even more pumped up than before. He banged his steering wheel, blew his horn and yelled out like a person out of his mind. One would have thought it was just another dog.

Off white marble flooring, comfy dark brown leather couch, glossy coffee table, sixty four inch television screen, two huge flower vases with bright flowers lay beside the start of two staircases leading to the first floor. Family pictures and paintings hung at regular intervals all along the walls. False ceiling with bright lights illuminated the living room. A huge chandelier at the centre hung out with tiny dazzling golden lights. Everything was expensive and incongruous. Still a new comer would be lost in this expensive decor, not Aavi.

On the couch sat Onik and Misty, relaxed and affixed to the television set deliberately avoiding Aavi who stood directly off their back at the entrance. Instead of being scared or running off to somewhere or showing any sort of reaction, Onik and Misty didn't move a muscle even after Aavi locked everyone in.

What are these idiots doing? Do they think we are going to have a chat about it?

In a trice Aavi had his right arm around Onik's neck. He locked him in and pulled him off the couch effortlessly with one quick jerk. The couch creaked back with Misty's weight on the support and crashed on to the floor as did Misty. He put out his hands trying to minimize the damage and in turn felt his body weight right through his arm. Meanwhile Aavi shook Onik with his biceps trying to squeeze away the life out of him. Onik mumbled for help. Misty emptied the massive vase and charged towards Aavi in spite of the jolt of pain he had felt. Misty's effort to hit Aavi from the back failed, he couldn't get past the enormous and agile Aavi. Not being able to see a way past and judging by how crimsoned Onik's face looked Misty didn't wait and threw the vase above Aavi's head. The vase made a striking and smashing sound, enough for Aavi to get startled and loosen his grip. Onik slipped out from the clutches of death and scrambled towards Misty.

A gun was being pointed at Aavi by Onik, who was now bold and complacent, Misty the observer.

"What a pity! You won't be able to avenge your mother. Take a step forward and I will blow you to bits."

The conviction in his voice made Aavi take a few steps backward. He missed an opportunity to end the drama.

"My Dad's a criminal. He is meant to hurt others, it's expected. It's in his blood. He does whatever the fuck he wants and there's literally no one that could tell him NO. Cheating and hurting my mom is where I draw the line. Unlike your mom Aavi, my mother doesn't go out and fuck someone else's husband. Do you have any idea what this does to a family? On top of that she had the audacity to do it right in our house, right in my parent's bedroom. If that wasn't enough she even spent the night. That morning I found out and I took a pledge to destroy that person.

My mom soon found out when one of her jewellery was missing. The fucking asshole gave it to his mistress, your hoe of a mother. My mom doesn't even stay here anymore. She has been kicked out from her own home, separated from her own child. Today's their anniversary and some sense had come to my Dad a few days ago. He went to get her back and tonight they are enjoying a nice dinner somewhere rich which the likes of you couldn't even dream of. I see a future for them now though it's not a certainty. I have to remove the rose and its thorn from their life. Not only remove but crush it completely." Onik became emotional and was laying out all that was in his heart and mind.

"What a surprise for me to find out that the rose's bud is a killer, *a child killer.* I was only going to push that poor girlfriend of mine, hurt myself and play the victim before the police. With them being on my Dad's payroll you would have been formally charged for her death. It was a simple and short plan. Luck wouldn't have it." Onik gave a disappointing look.

"Everything changed at the bridge. Misty was an anomaly to the plan. I had to be proactive. I had to grow up then and there. So I did. And here we are a trigger away from laying everything to rest, goodbye, you son of a whore." Onik fired, Aavi ducked and Misty covered his ears.

Onik missed a six foot target from ten yards. The gravity of it didn't even settle on him and Aavi darted at him and seized his neck. Onik couldn't move an inch. He was affixed to the floor by Aavi's weight and strength. The colour of his life was washed away and all that remained was darkness.

Misty didn't budge. There wasn't a way out. He wasn't looking for one. A while earlier he told his wife the truth about who he was and what he had done. It wasn't easy to tell nor was it a pleasant conversation. He had to do it over the phone. Facing her meant the possibility of seeing his daughter. A slight gaze would turn his mind. It was difficult but necessary.

"Why? Why did you do all of this? Why did you help him?" Aavi looked distraught.

"He would have done that anyways. I didn't take any part in it. I only witnessed. I didn't help Onik in his journey ever. He used me. I let him. I was enjoying being played around and experiencing new things. The kid had guts I never had. He liberated me. I had clung to you like I always did. You have no idea do you?" Misty took to the couch, palpitating.

"I was in love with you from the day I noticed you in the eighth grade. I discovered a year ago who I was. It's not easy to accept yourself and it's not easy to love yourself or our kind when the majority loathes us for reasons they themselves don't know. It's hard to accept what isn't generally accepted."

"The boys in our class were all fools. Girls I could care less about. And you were there, a cliché, tall, dark and handsome. Oh so very handsome. I couldn't take my eyes of you and yet I had to. You were so quiet and so alone, always alone. Not a flicker of smile on you. Not sad. Not happy, impassive."

"Something changed within you one day. You expressed a hint of exasperation and anger though only to yourself. You didn't take it out on anyone and I couldn't bear to see you in that state. I had to find the cause for this new-born reaction of yours. I followed you after school for weeks and eventually found out."

"I was the one who told Roy about your mom. You had so much within you to express my love and you did fantastically. It was supposed to be our first meeting, a new friendship and more."

"I paid heavily for what I did, an absolute injustice to me. My parents died in a car crash. I was supposed to go after you, console you and maybe embrace you, kindle a romance. Everything was put to halt indefinitely. My heart broke into a million pieces literally, the loss of parents and the loss of my first and only love on the same day and at the same time. How much can a kid take? And that too for someone who has always been scared of the people around him."

"Maths interested me. It consumed a lot of my time. The hours without it was the issue. Negative thoughts overflew my mind and everything sinister danced in my head. I began killing. Inflicting pain in this world the way it did to me."

"Then the coincidence of meeting you happens, lost feelings resurfaces and a sudden hate along with it. It wasn't the love of an innocent. It was now a love of a hateful person."

"I was extremely lucky that it was you who discovered me instead of some stray dog. Can you imagine me fighting it off? I would have been all bones by now. I used you. I had to use you. It became even easier when I saw the same loneliness shimmer in your eyes. I still do love you and for reasons unknown I hate you. Seeing you hurt makes me happy. What a twisted lover I am." Misty gazed at Aavi who was unmoved and had the same zeal about him as he had when he entered Onik's house.

"Why did I let Onik do what he did? He told me about his mom's misery due to yours. Irrespective of her not being the only one in the wrong I couldn't say no to him. I would have done something similar if it was me instead of

Onik."

"I'm disappointed in you though. Roy only insulted your mom and faced a harsher fate than Onik who actually defiled her."

"That's enough," said Aavi.

"It's the truth Aavi. You literally tore up our principal. There's a beast inside you, lurking at the edge of your soul. I keep trying to let it out and you are afraid of it showing you your true colour."

I could have been a rainbow. You pushed for red. You got red. And now I will smear you in crimson.

CHAPTER THIRTY-ONE

Half asleep half-awake Dinaat found it difficult to grasp the words from the phone.

"Hello... Sir.... Hello."

"Hmm..."

"The sound of a crash and a bullet firing was heard at Shaanu's."

Why do we need to clean up his mess?

"Hello... Sir... Hello." The voice was searching for Dinaat.

"I'll be there in half an hour or so. Get the rest of them meanwhile. Don't enter the premise and if any locals are gathered keep them at bay." Dinaat hung up.

The perks of the job, break your sleepless sleep for a crook.

Upon entering Shaanu's house there were pieces of a broken vase to either side of the door and to the front where the door wouldn't reach. Further away was a dead body, clearly strangled. Eighteen to nineteen years on him, Shaanu's Son? Family portraits on the wall confirmed the identity. At a greater distance awaited a horror show.

Unknown man lay in his own pool of blood, skinny to the bone and stripped naked. No items to identify. Few sharp pieces of the shattered vase were used to pierce the body, dismissed as an intruder or the assailant. Upon close inspection strangulation was confirmed as the reason of death. The cuts made posthumous strongly suggested a relation between the victim and the murderer and some unresolved anger towards the victim or the world.

A few drops of blood found its way up the stairs. The rooms were left wide open. The drawers and wardrobe of the master bedroom and what seemed to be the guest bedroom were intact. They were all locked and the murderer didn't put any effort into unlocking it. Shaanu's son's room was ransacked. What was stolen and how much was stolen was unknown. It seemed like a last minute ruse to make it look like a failed robbery.

Dinaat was unsettled. Someone had the audacity to directly take on Shaanu. It wasn't a declaration of war as there weren't any other gang members present, a personal beef?

Aavi..?

Possible but it would be a farfetched idea. Reena and Shaanu had been going on for a while. This could have been rational at the start, not now, unless Shaanu's done something to Reena. Dinaat noted to check up on Reena.

The resentment Dinaat had for Shaanu couldn't overpower the killing of his son. Children are children, whosoevers. Far too many crimes were being carried out. What was fearsome was the ease with which it was being carried out one after another in such a short span of time with no substantial witness.

Shaanu's location was unknown and his men wouldn't utter a word. They came here not long before Dinaat arrived and prevented any sort of crowd gathering. It was clear that they had been instructed to not make the whole scene a circus. Dinaat called them to identify the John Doe and they were in the blind as much as Dinaat. It took some effort to drive them out.

Once there wasn't anything left to do at the crime scene Dinaat left for Aavi's. The door was unlocked and no one was at home. Aavi's room was neat and tidy. Reena's bed was unkept and her wardrobe cleared out. This made no sense to Dinaat. He couldn't make a connection out of all this. Why did Reena leave? Has Aavi gone after her? Shaanu should be after the killer and who the hell is that John Doe? All these people could be tied up in this or none at all. Dinaat was, to say the least, flummoxed.

CHAPTER THIRTY-TWO

"Mom," said Aavi gently.

Reena had to strain her neck to look up to her son. Her eyes were sore and she looked drab and blank. Nothing changed on realizing there was an empty suitcase on her bed.

"You are leaving. I'm putting you on the first train. When you feel like getting out, do it. This...," Aavi put some of the stolen jewelleries and cash inside the suitcase, "use it wisely. You are smart, Mom. Find a way to live."

Did she have a photo of Aavi in her trolley? She didn't pack it. Aavi didn't put it. No. Did she need it to remember him? No. Could she forget her own son's face over time? It cannot be possible, right? It would be unjust.

Reena shifted her body to lean against the icy window seat. Her sleeping co passenger relaxed in her slumber and her hand fell out very close to Reena's thigh. It drew Reena's attention. She would rather ram herself into spikes than touch another human being. The bogies were nearly all occupied. No two adjacent seats were vacant. Reena had searched quite a number of bogies before deciding to settle.

The train was now at a halt for about fifteen minutes way past its two minutes stoppage time. The platform was deserted. There weren't any food or book stalls unlike in the towns and cities. Aavi didn't change the blood stained jacket and donned it casually out in the open. His face was serene. His body relaxed. He was in no hurry.

The train whistled. Reena had to say it now. What was it with her and her vocal cords? They simply ceased function.

"Aavi," weakly she said.

"Yes Mom."

"Do you have a photo of you?"

Aavi took out his wallet. There was a picture of him in his early teen, a subtle smile on him, short hair and innocent.

CHAPTER THIRTY-THREE

Meet me at the abandoned bridge, the bridge of connectivity. Once you spot my Otto, keep walking. Aavi's unexpected text from an hour ago read. Dinaat assumed he got his number from the card he left behind when he had visited Reena. It took a moment for Dinaat to register the place Aavi was talking about, then it him, the forsaken place. Perfect place for a crime... Why didn't he think of it?

He had set off in trepidation as to what he would discover, the principal, the girl, her father, Roy, Sukanya and worse many more of missing and unreported beings. He didn't call for back up nor did he report it to anyone else. There was an ultimatum to the text. An end to everything that was disturbing.

Fear of life was always out of the question and without a family it was absurd and illogical.

Dinaat stopped and stepped out of his vehicle when he came across Aavi's auto parked under a humongous banyan tree. He examined the auto and found nothing substantial. Then he took the empty road ahead hoping it would be a short walk.

Five minutes past, Dinaat spotted a shiny black SUV. *Shaanu's... There's going to be a mess, should have brought back up. Fuck!*

Dinaat hurried. When he got to the foot of the bridge, Shaanu had Aavi pinned to the ground. He was reaching for the stone nearby.

"Don't do it Shaanu." Dinaat interrupted the attempt to murder. He had his gun pointed at Shaanu steadily.

"He killed my son." Shaanu wailed.

"I know it's difficult to let him go. You have to let the law enforcement handle it. He will be hanged. Else you die here while your son's killer lives longer than you." Dinaat chose his words carefully.

Aavi murmured something and Shaanu who had almost let go of the stone grabbed it and went for the kill.

Three quick fire shots and the grieving thug went down with an unfinished vengeance.

CHAPTER THIRTY-FOUR

Aavi was jaded, contused, defeated yet cheerful. He took in the warm rays of the morning sun with deep long breaths. Last morning and now, the son and father knocked seven bells out of him. They were both dead.

Shaanu overpowered him. Aavi had taken on a raging bull whilst his wrath was extinguished. A pool of his blood should have stained the abandoned bridge. Dinaat intervened at the right moment.

"Did you text him too?"

"Ya..."

"All part of your crooked plans."

"Aren't you glad he's dead?"

"Yes." Dinaat wasn't ashamed to admit the bitter truth. No one else being here made it easier. "I have to arrest you, Aavi."

"Aren't you curious to know what transpired in our peaceful village? What tide came in and threw in so much chaos?"

"We can do that when you are behind bars."

"I may not talk. Right now I'm vulnerable and ready to be foolish enough to confess. I will keep it brief."

Dinaat was aware of Aavi playing him. Was he ready to take that chance?

"Speak."

"The unidentified person in Shaanu's home, I loved him and he used it against me. Don't look at me like that. I'm gay. It's not a crime." Any other day and Aavi would have been terrified to say his truth.

"Sorry."

"Keep it yourself. Nothing better can be expected by the likes of you. People in general, truth be told."

Dinaat's repulsive expression almost made Aavi act on his killer instinct. He let go of it as quickly as it rose. Aavi took a minute.

"I used to bring teenage couples here to give them privacy. It was easy money. I met Misty here. He was on other side of the bridge killing an innocent child. I went to stop it. He knew my secret. He was my classmate who was ostensibly in love with me as he claimed during those days. He leveraged me as to outing me out. I was scared of being discovered and facing inhumane consequences. At that time I didn't have in it me to kill him. I should have."

"I joined him and committed numerous crimes. You need to excavate this whole area. You will find them and a lot more and a promotion." Aavi grinned. Dinaat had a dreadful question. *How many?*

"Misty was from the other village. He usually picked up vagrant children. He's been killing for quite a number of years. He has a wife and kid. Take it easy on them."

Terror reigned over Dinaat. *Years!*

"The girl from the school was pushed of this very bridge by Onik, Shaanu's son. He pre-planned it and was going to frame me for her murder with the aid of his Dad and his connections. Misty's presence saved me. Framing me would have been better than what I set out to do."

"The trio of us were involved in some of it together. The principal was all of my doing. I don't regret the principal,

Onik and Misty. These three deserved it. I will not say why."

Reena..?

The second Dinaat started contemplating Aavi was onto him and snatched away his deadly revolver. Aavi intentionally didn't back away and let Dinaat fight to regain his lost possession. It was too easy for Aavi to dramatize it. Dinaat was lighter compared to Shaanu even with his sizeable belly.

Soon they both had their hands on the trigger with Dinaat fighting for survival and justice for all those inhumed and Aavi for his liberty. Then the revolver unloaded a bullet.

"Huh!" Aavi gasped. The cage finally crumbled to dust. He wasn't even aware that he was withheld. An illusive colour had sneaked in putting all its effort to destroy Aavi's identity. His shade was stronger than he could ever have anticipated. The serpent was put to rest. The seal was broken and he was free to wander and be himself.

www.ingramcontent.com/pod-product-compliance
Lightning Source LLC
LaVergne TN
LVHW041026150826
845672LV00001B/214

* 9 7 9 8 8 9 1 3 3 5 9 8 1 *